BETWEEN THE COVERS
AN ADULT ROMANCE ANTHOLOGY

SUZANNE BAGINSKIE   SHARI HELD   BRUCE PRATT
MAHENDRA WAGHELA   MARTHA PATTERSON
DIANE KANE   ASH ORLANDO   NICHOLE BLAKE
O'LABUMI BROWNE   JIM TRITTEN   SANDI HOOVER
CHRIS ALLEN   MAUREEN COOKE   RIZWAN ASAD

between the covers – An Adult Romance Anthology

Copyright © 2021 by JK Larkin

All rights reserved

Published by Red Penguin Books

Bellerose Village, New York

Library of Congress Control Number: 2021915206

ISBN

Print 978-1-63777-124-2

Digital 978-1-63777-125-9

No part of this book may be reproduced in any form or by any electronic or mechanical means, including information storage and retrieval systems, without written permission from the author, except for the use of brief quotations in a book review.

CONTENTS

BOYS AND OTHER TOYS Shari Held	1
BREAKING AND ENTERING Bruce Pratt	13
THE LIST Diane Kane	23
A WELCOME PROPOSAL Martha Patterson	39
RED DIRT COWBOY Ash Orlando	43
LE PAIN DE L'AMORE Nichole Blake	53
ENOUGH TO KILL Jim Tritten and Sandi Hoover	67
A TRIANGLE WITH TWO SIDES Mahendra Waghela	77
LOVERS IN HIDING Suzanne Baginskie	85
ROMANCE ON THE IRONHORSE O'labumi Browne	99
TO BEGIN AGAIN Chris Allen, Maureen Cooke, and Jim Tritten	105
THE OTHER MAN Rizwan Asad	121
About the Authors	133
About the Editor	139
Also from The Red Penguin Collection	141

BOYS AND OTHER TOYS

SHARI HELD

Friday night. Dean couldn't wait to get out of his suit and into his usual duds, a flannel shirt and well-worn jeans. It had been one of those weeks. One of those months, actually.

He grabbed his mail from the apartment community mail center and headed upstairs. October had begun on a sour note when his girlfriend Stephie – make that ex-girlfriend – confessed she'd been getting a little on the side. It hadn't bothered him that much. After all, he'd been tempted to hit on a girl he'd met at Buckaroo Bill's a few weeks ago. One more Bud and he'd have been a goner. Mistakes happen. He was a big enough man to acknowledge human frailty and forgive and forget.

His magnanimous attitude burst into flames when Stephie informed him her lover was a nurse where she worked. A female nurse named Brianna. Talk about a bruised ego. Dean shook his head at the memory. Still, he'd tried to suck it up. Joked about it to hide his injured pride.

It was the wisecrack about him getting a front row seat to watch them go at it that was a joke too far for Stephie. Next thing he knew, she'd thrown his key at him, gathered all her stuff down to their shared tube of toothpaste, and slammed the front door so hard the head on his beer dissolved like their doomed relationship.

Women. Can't live with them. Can't live without them.

Dean got changed, poured a beer, and sank into his cushy leather sofa to sort his mail – half bills, half junk – except for the package. He saved it for last.

He ripped open the brown paper wrapper, wadded it up, threw it in the trash, and opened the box. "What the hell!" Dean dropped it as if it contained a six-foot, writhing copperhead instead of a ten-inch purple sex toy. The pamphlet inside proclaimed it was a Raunchy Rabbit, guaranteed to make a girl orgasm both internally and externally in thirty seconds flat!

Geejuz! How the heck is a guy supposed to compete with something like that?

But the big question was: Who sent it to him? Snyder in the tech department? Cooper in accounting? Nah. They were both too cheap. Besides, they wouldn't pass up a chance to see him open it at work where the embarrassment factor would register off the charts. Must have been sent to someone else and he'd grabbed it by mistake.

He rummaged through his trash to confirm the address on the wrapper. Damn! Of all the days to have remembered to clean the coffee filter. The wrapping paper was covered in wet grounds. The label was smudged so badly he could barely decipher the address.

Double damn! It was for apartment 1-A. That meant it belonged to his new neighbor. He'd only met her once or twice in passing. She sure was a looker. Big green eyes, curly blond hair, and a smile any red-blooded male would have to be dead to ignore. But he couldn't remember her first, much less her last, name. And she hadn't yet put it in her mailbox. No way he could rewrap the box, address it to her, and stick it back in the mail center.

Dean paced the floor, trying to think. He handled logistics all day at work. It shouldn't be that big a deal. Try as he might, though, he couldn't figure out a way to give the unwrapped package to his neighbor. Short of, well, just giving it to her.

He could only imagine how that would go down.

"Sorry, ma'am but I accidentally opened your Raunchy Rabbit

by mistake. Hope it didn't inconvenience you any to wait another day for that Big O it promises to deliver. By the way, if you ever want the real deal, I'm right upstairs in 1-C. Happy to oblige."

He shook his head. Not gonna happen. He'd sooner pull his short hairs out with tweezers than have his first interaction with the girl in 1-A go down like that. Talk about losing the game before it even began. Nah, he was going to sit tight and do what he did best. Nothing.

He glared at the Raunchy Rabbit, then stuck it under a pillow on his couch so he wouldn't have to look at it and went to the kitchen for another Bud.

Maybe I should just get a dog.

Lily Rogers, the girl in 1-A, pursed her lips. The treat she'd ordered hadn't arrived as promised. Her work week had been brutal, and she'd really been counting on the sex toy to help her unwind. After all, a glass of drugstore bubbly and a bubble bath could only take a girl so far. Nothing relaxed her like an orgasm, and she hadn't had one of those for longer than she'd care to admit. As long as she kept it charged – and she'd make sure of that – it would be a reliable source of orgasms. And unlike men, the Raunchy Rabbit came with a guarantee.

Lily was new to Indianapolis. She knew no one, so her social life was non-existent. If this past week at work was indicative of future work weeks, she wouldn't have time to meet anyone. The guy upstairs in 1-C was kind of cute, but he was probably spoken for. Besides, dating a neighbor wouldn't be smart, even if his slightly longish blonde hair, chocolate brown eyes, and deep dimples tempted her. She poured her champagne and ran her bath.

Maybe I should just get a cat.

Saturday mornings Dean reserved for his workout. He had a weight bench and routinely pressed 200 pounds, 250 on a good day. He'd barely finished when someone knocked on his door.

He opened it to see his new neighbor standing there.

Oops! What if she knows I took her toy!

Dean just stood there.

"Are you going to ask me in?" she finally asked.

Dean's face reddened. "Of course." He opened the door wide and picked up two beer cans off the coffee table and shoved them in the trash. He pointed toward the couch. "Have a seat."

"I don't know if you remember me. I'm Lily, your new neighbor."

"Sure, I remember you," he said. "How's it going? All settled in after the move?"

"Well enough to make brownies." She smiled and eased back on the couch.

Dean glimpsed a flash of purple.

Damn! The Raunchy Rabbit. Oh, god! Please don't let her find it!

He had to get rid of Lily fast before that could happen. "What can I do for you?" he said, not sitting down beside her.

"I wanted to ask if I could borrow that proverbial cup of sugar."

Dean looked puzzled.

"For the brownies. I started on them and realized I don't have any sugar. I hoped you would have some."

"Oh. Sure." He rummaged through his kitchen cabinet, found an unopened four-pound bag of Domino's sugar, and handed it to her. "Here you go," he said as he walked toward the door and opened it.

After she left, Dean breathed a sigh of relief. Lily hadn't seen it, even though about two inches of purple had escaped from under the pillow. Of course, he'd hustled her out so fast he'd probably ruined his chances with her. But that was a small sacrifice to make to save face. And with his track record, he'd probably screw everything up anyway.

An hour later his bro Joe came by. Over a Bud and a foot-long sub, Dean told Joe about Lily and the Raunchy Rabbit.

Joe laughed. "You're smitten, my friend," he said. "I think it's time we paid a visit to your neighbor. We'll put you out of your misery, one way or the other. He retrieved the Raunchy Rabbit from its hiding place, opened Dean's door, and sprang down the stairs, brandishing the sex toy in front of him.

What the heck, Joe! Oh, god. Please, let her not be home!

Dean bounded after him and grabbed the offensive item from Joe just as Lily opened her door. He wanted to melt on the spot like the Wicked Witch of the West.

Lily took in the situation immediately. "What's with you?" she said. "Are you like about ten?" She snatched the Raunchy Rabbit from Dean. "Don't you know that taking someone's mail is a felony?"

She slammed the door so hard the windows at the end of the hall rattled.

Dean didn't want to risk running into Lily, so he didn't venture out during the remainder of the weekend. He spent time online trying to confirm if what she'd said was true. Was taking her mail, even if it was by mistake, a felony? The best he could figure out is that it could go either way. He'd just try to avoid Lily and hope for the best. Heck, maybe she'd use the damn thing and her mood would improve so much she'd forget all about coming after him on a felony charge.

On Monday morning Dean couldn't hide out any longer. He ducked his head out the door and saw the coast was clear. He checked his herringbone suit jacket for crumbs one last time before heading out his door. All was fine until he hit the bottom step. That's when Lily's door opened.

She was wearing a suit, too. But hers was a policeman's dress blues. And a gun hung around her waist. A big one.

Dean nodded in her direction, sprinted to his car, and took off before she could mention that felony thing again.

A cop! Son of a bitch! Son of a bitch! Can't a guy get a break? I'm going to kick Joe's butt for this.

"You look pretty preoccupied," Joe said during their coffee break at work. A mischievous look flitted across his face. "You see Lily this weekend?"

"Oh, yeah. I saw her all right. This morning."

"Was she wearing a big smile?"

"No. She was wearing a police uniform."

Joe almost spit his Columbian brew down the front of his grey shirt. "You've got to be joking."

"I wish I were. She's probably going to walk through the door any minute now and arrest me. In front of everyone." Dean shrugged his shoulders. "Thanks a lot, bro. If it weren't for you, she'd never know I had her, um, property and I wouldn't have to worry about getting arrested."

"You really think she'd do that? Your brains are clearly scrambled, my friend. I seriously doubt she'd risk all the blowback, all the embarrassment of having her precinct know she ordered a sex toy."

Dean's shoulders dropped two inches as he relaxed for the first time in a couple days. Joe had a point. He was probably in the clear. Still, he wasn't going to invite her over for a beer any time soon.

Lily never knew what made her look behind the trash container in the parking lot behind the precinct. It couldn't have been the faint mewl from the tiny black-and-white kitten, could it? Maybe. More likely it was her spidey sense. She picked up the shivering kitten and its claws latched onto her jacket as tightly as the jaws of death.

"Well, I thought about getting a cat. I guess you'll do." She lifted its tail. "How do you like the name Cruiser, little guy?"

The kitten meowed and snuggled under her armpit.

"I'll take that as a yes."

On the way home, Lily stopped at the pet store and picked up kitten food, a litter box and litter, kitty shampoo, and a small cat carrier. When they arrived, Lily gave Cruiser a bath and gently dried him off. She laid him on a towel while she got his food ready. When she turned to give it to him, he was fast asleep.

Over the next few weeks, Lily and Cruiser bonded. It was nice to have someone to come home to. Someone to talk to who never criticized her for gaining an extra pound or two or for spending too much money on a date dress she'd probably never wear.

"You're such a cute little goofus," she said, as she rubbed Cruiser's head. "Who needs a man with you around?"

Lily only wished that were true. She'd been mortified when Dean and his friend had shown up at her door, her Raunchy Rabbit in hand. She'd done her best to avoid running into Dean in the following weeks. She wished she hadn't gone all-out cop on him. Charging him with a felony? Really? No wonder she rarely had a date.

Why couldn't she just have said she'd bought the vibrator as a gag gift for a wedding shower? Nobody would get embarrassed. She would have invited them in. Dean's friend would have bowed out and left her and Dean. They would talk and get to know one another. Maybe he'd even invite her to dinner. Who knows where it could have gone from there.

She sighed. Who was she kidding? That scenario was for normal people. At twenty-two, she was one of the youngest police officers on the force. It was downright difficult for a female cop to find good dating material. The weird, unpredictable hours were deadly on a relationship. Most guys she'd dated couldn't take it long-term. That left the pistol sniffers – guys that get off on dating a woman in uniform who was packing.

Her dating life might be in the toilet, but it wasn't so bad she'd resort to dating one of them.

∼

It was dusk on a Friday night and Dean gathered his mail, then took the stairs two-by-two. Sitting on his welcome mat in front of his door was a tiny black-and-white kitten.

Dean reached down and scooped up the kitten to check for a collar. "What the heck? Where'd you come from, little guy?"

No collar. Dean put the kitten down. "You'd better get home, little guy. It's almost dark."

He unlocked his door and walked in. So did the kitten. "Hey, you can't come in here."

The kitten wasn't impressed. In response, it walked into the kitchen, sat in front of the refrigerator, and meowed.

"Okay. You must belong to somebody. You know what a refrigerator is. You want some milk?"

The kitten meowed.

"Okay. Just a bowl full. Then out you go. If any of my friends saw you, they'd make fun of my masculinity. You wouldn't want that, would you?" Dean served the kitten, changed into jeans, then grabbed a Bud and sat on his couch. When the kitten finished, it clawed its way up Dean's jeans to sit beside him and started purring.

"Whoa! What a big motor for such a little guy." Dean reached over and lifted it onto his lap, where it promptly fell asleep. He laid it on the couch, then found an empty box, put a towel in it, and placed the kitten inside. It didn't even wake up. He grabbed his keys and headed to PetSmart to buy the essentials.

When he got home, the kitten was awake, but hadn't left the box. When it saw Dean open a can of kitten food, it stretched and ambled over to its food bowl. While the kitten was eating, Dean set up the litter box.

"You know, cat, this is only temporary. When I do decide to get a pet, it's going to be a dog. A manly dog. A German Shepherd, maybe. Definitely *not* a kitten."

The next morning, Dean went to the community bulletin board to see if anyone had reported losing a kitten, but there was nothing. He went home and he and the little guy watched reruns of Buffy the Vampire Slayer.

Lily didn't like it one bit, but she was going to have to bite the bullet and ask Dean for help. Cruiser was missing. It wasn't time to feel self-conscious. Too much was at stake. She knocked on Dean's door more forcibly than she had intended.

"Who the heck can that be this early on a Sunday morning?" Dean stumbled out of bed, threw on his robe, and opened the door. "Hello."

"Hello," Lily said. "Sorry to bother you so early, but have you seen a black-and-white kitten?" She held her hands about eight inches apart. "About this big. His name's Cruiser." Her bottom lip trembled.

Dean smiled and beckoned for her to come inside. "I think I can help you out."

"Really? I'd be so grateful. There are a lot of doors to knock on…"

The kitten strolled into the living room, stretching and yawning. Ignoring both humans, he sauntered over to his food bowl and meowed.

"Cruiser!" Lily shouted as she ran over to the little guy. "Oh, thank god, you're okay." She picked him up, held him to her breast, and began stroking him. "I thought I'd lost you for sure."

Dean looked nervous. "Um, I didn't know he was yours. I found him in front of my door a couple nights ago and took him in. I looked at the bulletin board to see if anyone had reported him. Honest."

Lily resisted laughing. The poor guy probably thought she was going to accuse him of cat-nabbing. She decided to give him a break. "Thank you so much for taking him in. I've been working double shifts and barely managed to stop by to feed him a couple nights ago. He must have sneaked out behind me, and I didn't notice because I was rushing around. I didn't even know Cruiser was missing until this morning. I was frantic."

Dean appeared to be relieved. "No problem." He chucked Cruiser under his neck. "I'll get his stuff."

Lily watched as Dean gathered up Cruiser's food, bowls, scratching post, and toys. There were big balls and little balls, catnip mice, feathers on a cord, a floppy fish, a wiggly bug, and a cat string gizmo that attached to the doorknob.

"Seriously?" she questioned. "You've only had him two days."

Dean chuckled. "You aren't the only one in your family who likes toys."

Lily stiffened, a smart-ass retort on the tip of her tongue. Then her voice of reason took over. It was time she stopped letting the Raunchy Rabbit incident define their relationship.

She smiled instead. "Yes, we do."

Dean nodded in Cruiser's direction. "If you need someone to keep Cruiser occasionally, it would be no trouble. I'm all set up for it. And he's used to being here." As if to confirm what Dean had said, Cruiser rubbed against Dean's leg and started purring.

"Well, if you're sure it wouldn't be any trouble, that would be great."

They exchanged contact information and parted as, well, friends.

Lily practically skipped down the stairs. Things were looking up. "And I have you to thank," she said, giving Cruiser a big kiss on the top of his head.

~

Over the next few months, Cruiser came to visit Dean on a regular basis. When Lily came to pick up Cruiser, she'd stick around and they'd order take-out, play backgammon or watch TV, bitch about their jobs, squabble about which tennis player was the best ever, and even talk about their dreams.

It was unfamiliar territory for Dean. All his previous relationships had centered around drinking and sex. He couldn't be sure, but he thought he was in a relationship with Lily, the kind of relationship based on mutual respect and understanding. Whatever it was, he knew he didn't want to lose it. He didn't want to lose Lily and Cruiser.

Son of a gun! This must be love. But what if she doesn't feel the same way? What if she only sees me as her cat-sitter?

Dean shook his head. He didn't want to think about that. As far as he was concerned, it was time to take their relationship to the next level. Between the covers. Of course, then he'd be competing against the Raunchy Rabbit. His face crumbled. He'd be lucky to come in a close second.

Dean went downstairs to collect his mail – bills, ads, and a package wrapped in plain brown paper. He ripped the paper off and opened the box. And there it was. The Raunchy Rabbit. A note in Lily's handwriting was attached.

Dear Dean,

It's time for me to bid adieu to the rabbit in favor of you, the guy in 1-C.

The Raunchy Rabbit does live up to its reputation, but it falls far short when it comes to friendship, caring, and sexual attraction. So, I'm surrendering my Raunchy Rabbit to you in the hopes that you'll take me up on my invitation and take its place. Maybe I'm being presumptuous, but I hope not.

Anxiously awaiting your reply,
Lily

Dean's smile lit up the room.

Women. Can't live without them.

BREAKING AND ENTERING

BRUCE PRATT

Leaving the office for my noon appointment with the owner of *Stan The Man's Windows and Doors*, I got waylaid by Ed Marlin who said, "I'm hoping for a face to face on the Weathers' review this afternoon."

"Depends on when I get back," I said.

"It's important, Bill," Ed said.

Figuring it was Friday, and he'd let it go until Monday, I said, "Five-thirty work?"

"Great," he said, disguising any disappointment, "I'll be here."

Before he could delay me further, I snatched my briefcase from my desk, shoved my cell phone into my sport coat pocket and jogged down the stairs to the parking lot.

The morning's foggy cool had been baked away, the sky cloudless, the sun shimmering on the hood of my Camry, as I fired up the ignition and cranked the air.

For the past seven years, Gena and I have been restoring an 1865 farmhouse on Luther Hill Road, which sits astride a windy knoll on four of the original farm's fifty acres, and is flanked by new houses on either side. The bulk of the property, having been purchased by a local land trust, lies fallow. The last two years we've been focused on interior projects, but the spike in the cost of heating the place last winter spurred us to seek some quotes on replacing our drafty sash and pulley windows.

To avoid downtown at midday I swung south on River Road, but a mile before my turnoff traffic was halted both ways by an overturned log truck. In my haste to get away from Ed, I'd forgotten Stan's business card on my desk, but even if I'd had his number I had no cell service and my low battery light was flashing. By the time I'd circled back through town and pulled into my driveway, Stan was not to be found.

I hustled in the back door, plugged my cell into the charger, and grabbed the phonebook in the kitchen to look up Stan's number. As I was rifling the yellow pages, I heard voices from upstairs. Gena is forever forgetting to turn off lights or the radio, and I assumed it was the TV, which she'd been watching that morning while ironing her blouse.

When the voices grew louder, I tiptoed to the bottom of the stairs and intercepted not only the sighs and moans of a couple making love, but the unmistakable thump of the headboard against the guestroom wall. Panicked, I strode back into the kitchen and opened the door to the garage to look for Gena's car. When it wasn't there, I crept back to the hallway and peered out the front door window. The only vehicle on the street, other than my neighbor Tom Burnside's Jeep, was a gray minivan I didn't recognize.

For reasons I still can't explain, I succumbed to a visceral urge to load the 300 Savage I keep locked in the gun safe in the den before mounting the stairs. I made sure the safety was on and sidled up to the second floor, my blood surging against my skin. Five feet from the open guest room door I froze, as the throaty sounds of a man and a woman both on the verge of climaxing invaded my ears. Saliva flooded my mouth, and I drew a breath to steady myself, inhaling the scent of gun oil and stock polish. As I tried to quell the riot in my chest, the idea that Gena would be having an affair blistered my heart, but the possibility that she'd be screwing the window man forty-five minutes after she met him scorched my soul. With a final shout from the man, the bed ceased to creak, leaving only the rasp of winded lovers catching their breath.

I pictured Gena lying on her back, chest heaving, eyes closed, but wounded as I was by that vision, I found no point in shooting anyone over what had been to my ear consensual, though it did seem that a moment of terror was fair payback for the sting of such a betrayal. Cradling the rifle in my left arm, I stepped through the door and said, "The earth move?"

Tom Burnside burst up out of the tangled covers, blocking my view of the bed, and said, "Jesus, Bill, don't shoot."

"Why not?" I said, "Being neighbors give you the right to fuck my wife?"

Tom yanked back the covers, "It's Lynn," he said, pointing to his wife, breasts slick with sweat, black hair tangled around her face, hands groping for the duvet. As she gathered the covers back around her, Tom stood up, his shrinking weapon poking through the fly of his boxers. "I saw some guy on a ladder looking in your windows and came over to see what was up."

"And ended up screwing in our guestroom?" I said.

"It's part of our counseling," Tom said.

"Breaking into people's houses to have sex is part of your counseling?" I said. "Counseling for what?"

Lynn swung her legs over the side of the bed as she wrapped herself in the top sheet and said, "We didn't break in. Gena gave me a key when you guys were away last spring."

"And?" I said, when she paused.

"Our counselor told us to try sex in places we wouldn't normally," Lynn said, her eyes cast downward at her hands, which she was rubbing together as if they were cold, "Make love in the kitchen, rent an RV and drive to a romantic place for the weekend, things like that."

Lynn paused and stared at Tom, who was adjusting his fly, as if she expected him to speak, but he didn't respond. "I called Gena but she was showing a house, your office said you were out, and your cell went right to voicemail," Lynn said. "The guy seemed legit, but I decided we should be sure."

I slumped against the doorjamb and leaned the rifle against the hall wall. "A log truck wrecked on River Road," I said, "And I had to come all the way back around through town. That's why I missed Stan."

"We planned on getting everything back before you noticed," Tom said. "It was the peeping tom thing."

"Jesus Christ, Tom," Lynn said, tucking her hair behind her ears.

"What peeping tom?" I said.

"There isn't one," Tom said, "It's…"

"A fantasy," Lynn said, "We try to indulge each other's fantasies, but can we drop this? It's humiliating."

"What are you guys doing home now anyway?" I said.

Stepping into his pants, Tom said, "We meet at noon."

"For sex?" I asked.

"All right," Lynn said, slapping the covers gathered in her lap, "Jesus, yes, for sex. That's all you need to know, Bill."

"You tell Gena any of this?" I asked.

"Some," Lynn said, "Now please let me get dressed, I have to go back to work."

I shuffled downstairs and phoned Stan to apologize for missing him. "Saw what I needed," he said, "Though I think I scared your neighbors. At any rate, I'll have a quote for you by Monday."

Tom and Lynn ambled into the kitchen holding hands, the blue and white guest room sheets and a damp bath towel tucked under her arm. "I'm sorry," she said.

"No need," I said. "It's what the guest room's for."

"I'll bring these back tomorrow," Lynn said, handing the sheets and towel to Tom, "I have to run. I have a one-forty-five appointment, and I need to return that loaner van and pick up my car at Emerson's. Tell Gena, I'll call her."

After they left, I called my receptionist on my cell to tell her I wouldn't be back, then dialed Gena on the landline.

When Gena answered she said, "How did it go with the window guy?"

"He'll have a quote Monday," I said.

"He seem reliable?"

"Never met him," I said, "When I got here, Tom and Lynn had driven him off."

"What?" Gena said.

"Tom spied Stan on a ladder looking in the windows," I said, "And he and Lynn came over to see what he was doing. They hung around until he left, but Lynn wanted to be sure everything was fine inside the house."

"And?" Gena said.

"They were screwing in the guestroom when I got there."

"What?" she said, "You saw them?"

"Heard them first," I said, "Then I got my gun."

"Why the hell did you do that?" Gena said.

"I was worried that Stan was some creep," I said, "Or that you were having an affair."

"And you would have shot me?" Gena said.

"No, I wouldn't shoot anyone," I said.

"I told you I couldn't make it home, so why did you think it could have been me?"

"I don't know," I said, "But there was a minivan parked on the road and I imagined things."

"But you saw Tom and Lynn, having sex?" Gena said.

"Their counselor told them to make love in places they ordinarily wouldn't," I said.

Gena sighed, "Lynn told me they were seeing a counselor," she said, "But she didn't include that part."

"Tom mentioned a peeping tom fantasy," I said. "Lynn was mortified."

"I would think so," Gena said, the trace of a laugh bubbling in her voice.

"Tom didn't take his shorts off," I said, "And Lynn has a tiny rose tattooed on her left breast."

"Jesus, Bill. Talk about a peeping tom," Gena said.

"Not really," I said, "But can you come home?"

"No, why?" Gena said.

"So we can make love somewhere interesting."

"Bill," Gena said, just above a whisper, "I understand you're turned on by all of this, but I'm showing the Reeves' house at three-thirty. I'll be home by six."

"It's just one-twenty," I said, checking my watch, "We have plenty of time."

"That's romantic," Gena said, "Besides, don't you have things to do at the office?"

"I agreed to meet with Ed later," I said, "But it's never as important as he says it is."

"Deal with him this afternoon or he'll bug you over the weekend," she said. "I'm hanging up, see you at six."

Though she turned me down, Gena's never been the kind of wife my friends complain about, withdrawn or unenthusiastic, and I've often wondered if it's because we couldn't have kids that we've always found time and affection for each other. A spasm of regret scraped my heart, and I was ashamed that I had even considered that it could have been Gena in the guestroom. At the same I tried to fathom the searing depth of my grief if it had been.

I sat a minute in the kitchen, mulling over what Gena had said about Ed, and knew she was right, but as I'd skipped lunch I thought I'd see what we had in the house to eat before driving back to work. A *Post It* note on the refrigerator caught my eye—*What you don't put it in, you needn't work off in the gym*. Gena adores expressions and sayings, and I'd be retired if I had a sawbuck for each time I heard someone she's sold a house to repeat one of her pet phrases. Fingering the curled edge of the note, I wondered if she'd made it up herself or if it was something she'd read in a magazine, admiring the simplicity of the wisdom. I've borrowed plenty of her best adages myself, though when someone quotes the sign on Gena's desk that says, "A House Is Never A Home, Until There's A Family Inside," the irony pierces my heart. If I asked her why she'd stuck the note there, Gena would insist it was to inspire her to avoid snacking, but I knew it was to encourage me to workout, as my wife is the sole person I've encountered in this world who prefers a midmorning stalk of celery and glass of ice water to a lemon Danish and a latte. She runs before breakfast in all but the worst weather and takes aerobic classes at the health club when she can steal a few hours from work, while I'm lucky to muster enough motivation for forty-five minutes on the treadmill twice a week.

I wolfed down a tub of blueberry yogurt, then, taking a chance, drove back to the office by the River Road. The righted log truck lay on the shoulder with several flat tires, the remains of its mirrors glinting like ice in the sand along the edge of the road, the gouge of its spilled load ripped in the hillside, glimmering like a new wound. As I cruised into town, I made a mental list of the places I wanted to have sex with Gena over the weekend but realized I'd have been hard pressed to have made love that often in two days when I was nineteen, let alone at my age, and began to prioritize: the shaggy rug in the den, the leather recliner in the living room, the sunroom where, though we'd be hidden from view, our voices might carry to the ears of the Burnsides or the Dumonds if the windows were open and the breeze was right.

I coasted into my spot by the rear entrance to the office, left the windows cracked open, and braced myself to meet with Ed. My main gripe with him is that he treats the simplest policy review as if he were negotiating a nuclear weapons deal with the Pakistanis and refuses to use email for mundane matters, insisting on face to face meetings, but at sixty-two he's still my top producer, and it would kill Dad, from whom I inherited Ed along with *Belliveau and Sons Independent Insurance*, if I sent him packing before he was ready.

I gathered my messages from the receptionist, summoned Ed to my office, forced him to cut to the chase, and was on the road home in thirty minutes, though he made it clear he wasn't satisfied with the attention I'd given him. "I may need to call you about this later," he said, as I switched off my office lights and closed my briefcase, "We've had this account for thirty two years."

"And that's as long as you've been here," I said, "So you hardly need my advice on this."

Ed said, "If you say so," then spun out the door and trundled toward his office, and I could tell that he'd taken what I had meant to be a compliment as a dismissal of the importance of his concerns. I should be better at reading him, less matter of fact, but when I was a kid Ed was Mr. Marlin who worked for my father, then he was my co-worker, then one day, because I was the boss' only child, he became my employee, and I've never gotten used to that. My father understood how to make Ed feel important without patronizing him and you'd think after all these years I'd have figured it out as well, but I wasn't born with the same touch.

Gena had taken some chops out to thaw, but I stopped at *Gourmet to Go*, and purchased dinner for two: *Tournedos Provencal, Wild Herbed Rice, Fresh Green Beans with Almond Slivers,* and *Raspberry Cheesecake*, and picked up a bottle of Chianti and a split of Prosecco at *Reed's Wines and Spirits*. With real estate slow, Gena is at her office all the time working the phones, and I knew she'd appreciate the effort, even if she gave me some grief about the cost. She trudged through the front door a little after six, laid her briefcase on the chair in the hall, and inhaled a deep breath. "You didn't go back to the office?"

"I did," I said, "And I picked up dinner. We can grill the chops tomorrow."

"*Gourmet to Go?*" she said.

"It wasn't too bad," I said.

"I'm glad," she said, "I'm beat."

I kissed her and ran my hands up under her skirt. She stepped out of her heels, wobbling, momentarily lopsided in my embrace, and said, "Let me pee and change."

"No," I said, "Pee, then let me undress you."

A tiny laugh, almost a chuckle, escaped her lips. "Okay," she said, starting up the stairs. I picked up her shoes and trailed her to the second floor, nearly bumping into her when she stopped short at the top step. "Forgot to put your gun away," she said, "Must have scared the hell out of Tom and Lynn."

"I did," I said.

I sat on the edge of our bed, taking off my shoes and socks while

Gena used the head. She ambled out of the bathroom, dropped her pantyhose in the hamper, and grabbed a Hudson's Bay blanket from the cedar chest and tossed it on the bed.

I stood up. "Dance?" Gena said, unbuckling my belt.

I shucked my slacks and joined her in a slow two-step, completing one circuit of the bedroom, her bare feet resting on top of mine. As we passed back by the bed, we heard my cell phone ringing in my pant's pocket. "Five bucks it's Ed," Gena said.

"He can wait," I said, helping her out of her blazer and laying it on the bed behind me.

When I reached to unbutton her blouse, Gena grabbed my hands and leaned back, like a figure skater about to drop into a death spiral, and I stared into her black eyes. She tilted her head as if to get a different view of my face, pulled herself back to me, and reached into the fly of my shorts. With her other arm she snatched the blanket from the bed and said, "Lock up the gun, and I'll pull my car into the garage."

THE LIST

DIANE KANE

It was a smooth take-off out of Boston. I settled in for the long flight to Seattle and ordered a rum and coke, silently toasting my ex-boyfriend, who broke up with me on the way to the airport. After my second drink, I started to wallow in self-pity. I was twenty-nine years old, never married. I had wasted too much of my time on losers. When the lights of Chicago flickered below, I decided I wasn't settling for anything less than Mr. Perfect. With three hours left, I should have been making notes for my business meeting. Instead, I made a list.

1. Handsome.

No, cross that out, I told my drunken self. It sounds too shallow. Oh, hell, who cares, it's my list, and I want handsome as number one. Tall, blonde, and delicious.

2. Healthy.

Now that's not shallow. It's essential to have someone healthy for a long-term relationship. Not too buff, more like lean and lanky.

3. Gallant. Like heroic or brave? Yes, think Prince Charming, without the tights. I held the pen to my lip.

4. What about independent? Yes, I don't want a sniveling Mama's boy.

Independent (but not too bossy)
5. Honest…

One more rum and coke, and I passed out until the 'fasten seat belts for landing' announcement blared over the intercom.

∼

Seattle airport was bustling even at 4 am. I had a two-hour layover for my connecting flight to Anchorage, Alaska. It took me nearly all that time to get to my next plane. I raced through the corridors pulling my top-heavy carry-on behind me, stopping only for the ladies' room and a quick coffee and pastry. I could see my gate, and they were loading. I slid around a row of chairs and ran face-first into a large solid object covered in plaid flannel. My carry-on slammed into the back of my legs, and I fell backward on top of my red Samsonite. I heard a deep rolling laugher. Through my disheveled mass of red curls, I saw a bulky man with straight black hair, dark almond-shaped eyes, and a plaid flannel shirt.

"It's not funny," I said.

"That's a matter of opinion."

I untangled myself from my luggage and struggled to get up.

"Let me help you."

"I don't need your help. I have a plane to catch." Stomping off to my waiting flight, I glanced back with another glaring look and tripped over a rug. I heard his cruel laughter again. Finally settling into my seat, I tried to put the awful experience behind me.

Just as the tension in my neck faded, I felt a nudge to my knee. "This seat is taken," I said. There was another persistent poke. I pulled out my earbuds and looked into the face I hoped never to see again. "What do you want?"

"I was on standby. That seat is mine." The big lug pointed to the empty seat beside me. I studied his face while he tried to fit himself into the small space by the window. A broad, flat nose spread between high, prominent cheekbones. His bronze skin weathered and lined made him look older, but I guessed he was probably close to my age. If I had to spend the next two hours sitting next to this brute, I figured I might as well be courteous.

"My name's Rachel O'Brien." I held out my hand, but he didn't take it.

He smiled, but I saw no humor in his expression. "O'Brien, that's Irish, right?" he continued.

"Yes, full-blooded and proud of it," I said. "You're Alaskan?"

"What was your first clue?"

I hoped I hadn't offended him. "So, what's your name?"

His dark eyes were piercing. "Eagle's Pride."

"No, sah, you're kidding, right?"

"My grandfather was called Eagle. When I was born, my grandmother said that I would be his pride. Everyone calls me Pride."

"Wow, no wonder you're so arrogant."

"I'll take that as a compliment."

I decided to change the subject. "What do you do for work?"

"I do what almost everyone who lives on an island in Alaska does for work."

"You're a fisherman?"

"Good guess," he said. "So, what do you do?"

"I'm operations coordinator for the largest Logistics company on the east coast."

"Logistics, huh?"

"Yes, it means—"

"Getting things from here to there as fast as possible," he finished.

"Yes, you're right."

"I didn't go to a fancy highfalutin' school in Boston, but fishing has taught me a lot about business and trade. I also learned a great deal about life at the University of Mat-Su in Anchorage." His laugh was far-away and haunted.

"I didn't go to a highfaluting school. I attended the University of Massachusetts. I'm sure your school was a good one also."

"Yeah, it was very enlightening."

"By the way, how did you know I'm from Boston?"

"It's not 'hahd' to tell. We use R's in our words around here."

"Oh really, well, we use G's at the end of falutin' where I come from." I'd had enough of trying to make nice. "I hope you're not expecting any more conversation because I'm tired. I'm going to sleep, and I hope I don't do anything to make you laugh."

"I think that spectacle you made in the lobby was good enough to satisfy me for a while."

"Ugh."

"I planned on getting some sleep on this flight too. I spent the day in Seattle getting down and dirty with my new lady Charlotte. I'm pretty worn out."

"How disgusting."

"Charlotte is a beauty," he smirked. "She's my first."

"Oh please, spare me the details."

He laughed that annoying deep laugh again, and my face grew hot. Peeling off his plaid shirt, he crumbled it into a ball in his large hands and stuffed it behind his head. He closed his eyes, and it wasn't long before he was snoring.

To my relief, I parted ways with Pride in the teaming corridors of Anchorage Airport. Good riddance, I thought. I followed the signs that said Aleutian Air and navigated the long hallways. The signs got smaller and smaller as the corridors did the same. An arrow pointed to a one-person escalator that took me down into the sub-world of the airport. A female voice crackled over an intercom, and I tracked the sound. My flight was scheduled to depart at 10 am. It was a little past nine. I squeezed my carry-on through an aisle of plastic orange seats, tripping on random backpacks. I had settled into an empty seat when the intercom crackled to life, and the woman at the desk cleared her throat.

"All flights from Anchorage to Dutch Harbor are indefinitely postponed due to weather."

"Indefinitely," I said. "What the hell does that mean?"

"Indefinitely," the woman repeated. My voice was obviously

louder than I had thought. "Until further notice, for the unforeseeable future, a considerable amount of—"

"Alright," I said. "I get it."

I sunk back in my chair. "I don't even want to go to the godforsaken port of Dutch Harbor."

"Dutch Harbor is one of the most beautiful and remote parts of this country," a low chastising voice said from a seat behind me. "Very few people ever get to see it. You're extremely fortunate to have the opportunity to go there." I turned around to face the bane of my recent existence.

"You're like a bad penny," I said.

"Did you ever think that you might be the soiled penny?"

"I said bad, not soiled."

"Have you looked in the mirror lately?"

I dug through my purse and pulled out a mirror. I had left Boston eight hours and several rum and cokes ago. I looked terrible. "Is there a ladies' room in this poor excuse for a plane terminal?" He pointed across the hall.

"You clean up pretty good," Pride said when I returned. He was starting to give me the creeps.

A well-dressed guy sitting in the next row from us turned around. He looked at me and smiled. His blue eyes glimmered in the sun streaking through the dusty windows. His gaze moved deliberately toward Pride, and his face turned to stone. I felt Pride shift his large body and move to the edge of his seat.

"Wow, who's that?" I asked. "He looks like he might fit my list." Handsome, I thought.

"What list is that?"

"The one I made for the perfect guy."

"Weren't you ever told, never judge a book by its cover? He's more like the perfect asshole."

The gorgeous hunk of man made his way purposely to where Pride and I sat. "Excuse me, Ms., is everything all right here?"

His blue eyes, even more dazzling close-up, had me tongue-tied. "Yes, yes," I stuttered. "I, I think so."

He held out his hand. "Kyle Carrigan, with the Department of the Interior, United States Government."

I put my hand in his, and he grasped it firmly. "Rachel O'Brien," I said.

"Ah, I knew it when I saw that beautiful crimson hair." His smile was warm and genuine. "An Irish girl after my own Irish heart."

Pride made a slight gagging noise. Kyle turned his attention, never letting go of my hand.

"Pride, I didn't know you were out already," Kyle said through his perfectly straight white teeth.

"You didn't get the memo?"

"Are you going to Dutch, Ms. O'Brien?" he asked, turning back toward me.

"Why, yes, I am," I said. "Please, call me Rachel."

"My pleasure, Rachel. Perhaps you would like to take a walk with me," Kyle gently pulled my hand. I stood, and our bodies nearly touched in the narrow aisle. My five foot six inches topped out directly under his strong chin. His tailored white shirt and dark blue jacket fit like a glove on his long, lean body. Healthy, I thought.

"I'd love to," I said. I couldn't feel my feet touching the floor as he guided me out of the room.

"When I saw you with that loser Pride, I couldn't believe that a classy girl like you would give him the time of day. How do you know him?"

"Oh, I don't know him at all," I said. "I bumped into him in Seattle airport, and he seems to keep appearing wherever I go."

"He's nothing but trouble."

"What did you mean when you said you didn't know he was out already?"

"Out of prison."

"He was in prison? What for?"

"He was incarcerated six months at Mat-Su penitentiary in Anchorage for assault and battery."

"He told me that was where he went to school." My face flushed with anger.

"Some might call it a school if they were looking for an education in trouble. Pride's a con artist with an explosive temper. You're safe with me, darling."

Gallant, I thought. This guy fits my list perfectly.

"The department sends us out there every year on a humanitarian mission," Kyle explained. "We escort the native Unalaska Islanders out to their ancestral burial grounds on the far side of the island. We take pictures for the media, and everyone is happy." He smiled a silly smile, and I laughed. From where I was standing, I saw Pride turn to look in our direction.

The microphone crackled again at 4 pm, "Flight 20 from Anchorage to Dutch Harbor will be boarding at gate two in ten minutes." There was a stir of excitement. "We will be loading by priority."

"Priority? What does that mean?" I asked Kyle.

"No need to get your Irish up, Rachel. Priority means people of importance get on the first flight. It's your lucky day. You're with me."

"Wait, my carry-on."

"They'll send it tomorrow. This is a no luggage flight."

"What?"

"To make up for all the canceled flights today, they are filling up the plane with passengers out to the island. They put more seats in where they usually put cargo."

"But you have yours."

"One of the benefits of being with the government, darling."

As soon as we leveled out, the flight attendant unbuckled her seatbelt. She unhitched a cart from the wall and pushed it down the single aisle, stopping at each seat. "I could use a good stiff drink," I said.

"Well, you're not going to get one on this flight. Mountain Dew is the strongest beverage on that cart. I could use some alcohol myself," he said. "I'm buying when we get to The Grand Aleutian Hotel."

"That's a date." I smiled.

The driver who met us at the gate was a slight Asian man. He put all the luggage in the back of the van and silently drove us to the hotel. We crossed a bridge at a narrow part of the harbor and came to the first paved road I'd seen so far on the island. The buildings in this area were drab and with low profiles. In the distance, across a manicured area, lay a pond surrounded by tall ornamental grasses. On the other side loomed a three-story sprawling palace. The Grand Aleutian Hotel was an anomaly of grandeur in an otherwise bleak and barren landscape.

Kyle and I parted in the lobby with plans to meet later. I didn't have anything to unpack, so I checked out the amenities of my room. The luxurious bathroom proved to be a treasure trove of personal items. I took a long hot shower and used the whole sample-size bottle of tropical body wash. I toweled off and covered myself in cherry blossom lotion. Then I shook out my clothes and put them back on. At least I would smell good. I tingled with the mounting excitement of meeting Kyle in the lounge.

The wide, winding staircase that led down to the lobby made me feel like a princess, even in day-old clothes. I was relieved when Kyle came over as soon as I entered the lounge. Kyle looked me over with approving eyes and kissed my cheek lightly.

"I bet you're a margarita girl," Kyle said.

I'd never had one, but if he thought I was the type, then that was the drink I wanted. It wasn't bad, but a lot stronger than my usual watered-down choice. After another salty cocktail, I was getting a little woozy.

Kyle got up. "Where are you going?" I asked.

"You need another drink, darling."

I was still alert enough to know that I would be on the floor if I had one more margarita. "No, thank you. I have an appointment at the UniSea Processing Plant at 9 am tomorrow."

"The night is young, Rachel." I kept my composure and my will, barely.

"All right," he said. "I'll just go to the gym before I go to bed, then."

~

The following day, I woke early with a slight headache. I ordered a coffee and Danish from room service and felt a little better. I showered, redressed, and was about to go down to the lobby when there was a knock at my door. I opened the door with a smile, hoping it was Kyle, but it was the desk clerk. She handed me a bag of clean, neatly folded clothes, along with a thick warm coat.

"A nice-looking man asked me to give you these."

"Thank you."

I changed into neon pink and black leggings and a matching turtleneck tunic. They fit perfectly. I checked my look in the mirror. I liked it. The outfit was sexy and warm as well. I put the heavy coat over my arm and strutted down the hall.

The aging white transit van was waiting for me outside the hotel at 8 am. The same slight Asian man jumped out to hold the passenger door for me. "Howdy, ma'am." He had a large toothy smile. "Chan at your service." I was surprised at his well-spoken cheerful manner since he hadn't spoken at all on the ride the night before.

"I'm Rachel," I said. "Chan, is it?"

"My real name is too hard for most people to pronounce. Chan is my idol. So, everyone calls me Chan."

"It's a pleasure to meet you, Chan." His smile was infectious. "I have an appointment at the UniSea Processing Plant at 9 am, but first, would you mind bringing me to the airport? I'm hoping my luggage is there this morning."

"No problem Ms. Rachel."

"You drove me to the hotel yesterday," I said when I got in the passenger seat next to him.

"I remember. You were with the government man, but I knew

you were different." He started giving me a narrated tour of everything that we passed, and I didn't get a chance to ask him what he meant by 'different than him.'

We parked in the dirt parking lot in front of the airport and entered the terminal. I stood in the doorway to the luggage room with my hand over my mouth to stifle a scream. A pile of luggage towered nearly to the ceiling and spread out like a pyramid. A loud humming noise of a conveyor belt moving to the window on the far side of the room dropped luggage one by one from the gaping hole, adding to the pile.

"NO," I shouted.

"It's okay," Chan said. "What color is your luggage?"

"It's red with a yellow scarf attached to the handle," I sobbed.

"I'll find it." He dodged the falling luggage and burrowed into the pile. Moments later, he came out with a huge grin holding my red Samsonite. He blushed when I threw my arms around him and gave him a big hug.

"Thank you so much. Now I need to get to my appointment."

"No problem, Ms. Rachel. I'll bring you to the plant, and then I'll take your luggage to The Grand Aleutian."

"You're the best, Chan."

He dropped me off at the sprawling processing plant, and I followed the path toward the office door. The director welcomed me and showed me all the documentation on exports for the company I was representing.

"The barges come in on a random schedule from Seattle. I'm afraid we are hostage to their will," he said.

"Well, that seems to be our problem. How can we fix it?" I gathered more information, but I was puzzled as to how to fix the problem. I told him I would go over the data and agreed to meet again in a couple of days.

Chan returned for me at 2 pm.

"How was your day Ms. Rachel?" I explained the problem with the barges.

"Well," he said. "If the company wants their product faster, they should hire their own barges."

"Can they do that?"

"Sure, if they have enough money."

"If they can control the exporting, I bet they would think it was money well spent. Chan, you're a genius!"

"You're kind, Ms. Rachel."

"So, how was your day?" I asked him.

"Great, I saw my friend Pride this morning after I dropped you off."

"Huh, he's your friend?"

"Oh yes, but I haven't seen him in a while. He's been away."

"So, I heard."

"You know Pride? He's a great guy." I looked at Chan in disbelief. "He's always been a fisherman working on other people's boats. Now he's bought his own, and he's super excited."

"His own boat?"

"His grandfather, Eagle, died while Pride was away. They were real close. His grandfather left him some money and instructions that he wanted him to buy a fishing boat and become a captain. Pride went to Seattle to buy one, and he says she's a beauty."

"Really, what would the name of this boat be?"

"It's a woman's name. Let me think."

"Would it happen to be Charlotte?"

"Yes! That's it. How did you know?"

"I had a funny feeling." Not only was Pride a liar and a con artist, but he was also a mean bully. He led me to believe he was talking dirty about a real woman to make me uncomfortable.

Chan dropped me off at the front doors of The Grand Aleutian. I went to my room, where I found my luggage waiting for me like an old friend who had been through a harrowing ordeal and needed reassurance. I wiped off the grime as best I could and unpacked. In the outside pocket, I found my list. I read it over and smiled. I had found the perfect guy, and he was waiting for me downstairs. I slipped into some black leggings with a short pink skirt. I was thankful that I had made a last-minute decision to bring a sexy shirt. I put it on and checked my look in the full-length mirror. I've got this, I thought. I slowly descended the winding staircase in my two-inch heels and heard a long low whistle.

"Oh, darling," Kyle said. "I've got to be the luckiest guy in Dutch." He escorted me on his arm to the elegant dining room.

"There aren't any prices on these entrees."

"It's all market prices. Not to worry, the government is picking up this tab."

I told Kyle about my day at the plant and my adventures with Chan.

"You need to be more cautious with these locals, Rachel. They're born con-artists." I started to protest, but Kyle went on to tell me about his plans for the next day to go out to the burial grounds. "At least the weather is supposed to be good," he said. "It's tedious enough to herd these people out there without battling the incessant bad weather here."

"It sounds interesting. I'm not doing anything tomorrow. Do you think I could come along?"

Kyle hesitated. I was sure he was considering my well-being on such an arduous trip. "I have the warm clothes you got for me," I said. "I'll be fine."

"Warm clothes?"

"Yes, the desk clerk brought them to my room. She told me they were from a nice-looking man." Kyle looked tongue-tied. "They fit perfectly."

We polished off the bottle of champagne and ordered after-dinner liquors. Kyle steadied me as I wobbled my way to the lounge. A fisherman bumped me, and I spilled my drink. Kyle confronted the man.

I pulled at his tense arm. "It's all right," I said. "I just want to go up to my room anyway."

"That sounds good." Kyle put his arm around my waist, and I leaned into his firm body as we ascended the stairs. I opened my door and turned to say goodnight. He kissed me on the lips, and it took my breath away. When he pushed me against the door jamb with his body, it felt so good that I almost gave in. But I was still sober enough to know better.

"Kyle, no, not now." I was breathless.

"Are you turning me down again?"

"We've both had a little too much to drink. Let's sleep on this."

"That was my plan." He pulled me close, and I pushed back.

"I meant, let's sleep on this separately." I closed my door and leaned against it. I hoped I hadn't made the wrong decision.

The following day I showered and dressed in the warm outfit Kyle had given me.

When the van arrived, Kyle sat in the back with the camera crew and their equipment. I climbed in the front with Chan. On the ride, we talked about the ancestral pilgrimage. "There are three primary burial grounds on the far side of the island," he said. "Family means a lot to the people here."

"I can see that."

"My family is all gone, but the people here treat me like I'm one of them."

"I don't have a real family either," I said. "My parents died when I was nine. I grew up in foster homes." I didn't talk about my personal life with most people, but Chan was different. I turned around to see Kyle taking a long sip from a flask.

Chan dropped us off when we got to the state dock, where a Coast Guard boat awaited us. There were about two dozen Aleuts already aboard. I cringed when I saw that one of them was Pride.

We skirted the coast for another hour, and a small dock appeared in the distance. I stood by the railing, and a girl with straight jet-black hair stopped beside me.

"I'm glad you're wearing my coat today," she said. "It looks good on you."

"Your coat?" I asked as she headed for the ramp. I tried to catch up to her but got caught in the departing crowd. Kyle walked up to me, taking another sip from his flask.

"That girl said this was her coat." I tried to point out the girl in the crowd but couldn't find her.

"Rachel, I told you they're all con-artists. She's trying to get the coat from you. You're so gullible." I don't know why his words annoyed me; he was right.

The ATVs were lined up and running. Pride helped a senior woman and another woman into one of the vehicles. The young girl that spoke to me on the boat climbed in beside them.

I got in the back seat of another vehicle with Kyle. The driver proceeded slowly over rough terrain, following no apparent road. A large pile of stacked boards came into view in the distance and looked out of place in the natural landscape. We parked and gathered together. The group walked solemnly toward a small outcropping of rocks. It wasn't until I got close that I realized they were stone markers. Worn and weathered, most of the stones lay broken or indistinguishable.

After we visited the other two burial sites and many pictures were snapped, we turned to head back to the dock. The sun was low in the sky. Kyle had finished off his flask and fallen asleep as soon as we had returned to the ship.

Chan was waiting for us at the state dock in Dutch. It was a quiet ride back to The Grand Aleutian. I needed time to think. I went right up to my room, got into my nightgown, and ordered room service. There was a loud knock, and I opened the door expecting room service. Kyle slammed the door wide open with his fist and pushed me back into the room. He kicked the door shut.

"You're not going to tease me anymore, darling," he slurred and pushed me onto the bed. "I'm taking what you owe me."

"Stop, Kyle, no." I struggled to get out from underneath him. He pinned my arms to the bed and sucked on my neck and chest. I twisted and kicked.

"Stop fighting me, you little hussy." I freed one of my arms from his grip and slapped him across the face. Before I knew what hit me, the side of my head exploded with pain. Then his arm came across and hit me again from the other direction. I was barely hanging on to consciousness when I felt him rip my nightgown down the front.

There was a pounding on my door. "Go away," Kyle shouted.

"Help," I screamed weakly.

Out of my quickly swelling eye, I saw Chan. He took a karate pose with one leg up. "Kiah," he yelled.

Kyle punched him in the chest. Chan hurtled backward towards the door and smacked into a looming figure in the doorway.

"Pride," I sighed.

Two law enforcement officers pushed past him, with guns drawn.

Kyle staggered back and raised his arms. "I'm with the Federal Government."

"I know who you are," one of the officers said. "And you're under arrest."

"Are you okay?" the officer asked.

"Yes, thank you. You got here right in time."

"We'll need a statement from you sometime tomorrow, Ms.," the officer said. "You won't have to see him again."

Chan had come to my side. "Ms. Rachel, I'm sorry my karate isn't as good as it used to be."

"Chan, you're still the best to me."

"I had a bad feeling about that guy. He's the reason Pride went to jail."

"Really? What happened?"

"Last year during the outing, he touched Pride's sister inappropriately, and Pride punched him." Chan shook his head. "Pride was defending her honor, but the government didn't see it that way."

"Where is Pride now?" I asked.

"He said he had important business at the dock."

"Take me there." I glanced at the paper with my list on my nightstand.

"What's that?" Chan asked.

"A piece of trash," I said and threw it in the wastebasket.

"So, you're the good-looking guy who left the clean clothes for me at the hotel?" I asked Pride when I caught up to him.

"I knew you would need them since your luggage got delayed. Cera, my sister, is about your size. She was glad to help when I told her about you."

"I wondered where you went so fast."

"I'm sorry I had to leave, but I knew you were in good hands with Chan."

"So, Charlotte is here?"

He blushed. "Yes, I rented a space at the dock for her arrival."

"Can I meet her?"

"Sure." Pride beamed as he showed me around his new lady.

"She is a beauty," I said. "Pride, I'm sorry I was wrong about you."

"I'm not an easy person to read."

"You're a book that is a lot different than your cover." As we walked back to his truck, I tripped over a moss-covered stone, and Pride caught me.

"You fall a lot."

"I didn't until I met you."

"Well, I guess what they say is true."

"Oh really, what do they say?"

"Pride comes before the fall." Tears of amusement welled in the corner of his eyes as his deep laugh echoed across the bay. He was right, but I never imagined it would be me falling head over heels in love with him.

A WELCOME PROPOSAL

MARTHA PATTERSON

It was a Gothic manor house, on a lovely estate occupied by a gentleman and his two children whom I'd been employed to teach. I'd come from almost nothing – my father had been a coal miner – and I'd been casting about for some kind of work to do in a good household, and perhaps rise above my station. Having grown used to living in a shack with only hay for mattresses to sleep on, I aimed for something better. So I placed an advertisement in the papers to be a governess. Hardly knowing what to say about myself, with my humble background, I included the information that I had very good references.

The children's father, a widowed, aristocratic farmer, found me through my advertisement. The day I appeared for my interview, I was impressed by the stateliness of his home. Never before had I lived in such a place! And when we first met, I was impressed by his manners and eloquence and restraint. I knew he was still sad, for his wife had died only a year before, and people in the village said he'd never get over losing her.

I'd never had a spouse or lover myself, and could only imagine his deep distress. But he was eloquent and handsome, his children were dears, so sweet and compliant, and this man was so well-to-do

I couldn't imagine that I wouldn't enjoy my new position as governess in such an attractive house.

I began my post two weeks later. Things were going well and once Mr. Archer even asked me to dine with him. At dinner, I thought he must be lonely, for he kept glancing at the portrait of his wife upon the wall. I felt a little jealous of her – or, at least, of his memories of her. He was so good-looking and gracious. But things rapidly took a turn for the better.

I'd made friends with other servants in the household and my young charges seemed to like me. I took them for long walks through the wild moors of the estate and was charmed by their company. One day, when I'd just finished instructing the two children, a boy and girl aged eight and ten, in a French lesson, and had sent them off to their supper, their father entered the nursery room.

I was wearing a calico dress made of cotton and trimmed with lace – perfect for bodice-ripping, with my corset tightly laced beneath, but I had no expectations of such an event when Mr. Archer entered the room. How surprisingly I was deceived by his manner, which at first, at our initial interview to teach his children, had been so respectful and becoming of a restrained gentleman.

"My dear Lucy," he began. "I can't help noticing how fetching you look in that dress, and how well you seem to work with my children. They're already fond of you, and you've only been here two months!"

"It's nothing," I said, standing near the fireplace in the nursery, where the flames from the late afternoon fire were just beginning to dwindle. "They're wonderful babes – and good students. And I'm so pleased to be living in such a fine house as this!"

"My father left this house to me," Mr. Archer said, approaching me slowly. "But I also wanted to tell you how attractive you are to me, personally. You have such good manners and the firelight on your fair skin lights it up like the last flicker of sun shining against the clouds when it sets in summer."

I smiled modestly.

A WELCOME PROPOSAL

"I hope you're not being facetious, Mr. Archer," I answered. "My skin is fair because I stay *out* of the sun."

"Not facetious at all," he replied, "and please call me Roderick." He strode to the bookcase, took from it a volume of poetry, and fingered the pages.

"Do you like poems?" he asked.

"I do when they make sense – but sometimes they don't," I replied.

He replaced the antique book on the shelf.

"Then I won't bore you with poetry. But I'd love to kiss you."

With that, he approached, wrapped his arm around my waist, and planted a kiss upon my mouth.

"Sir!" I said, drawing away. "Do you think your behavior befits a gentleman of your stature?"

He pulled me closer and placed his swarthy, freckled hand upon my bosom.

"My God!" I cried, "Do you always do this with young women?"

"I never have before," he exclaimed back, "but I'm in love with you! And I'm asking you to marry me." He knelt at my feet in supplication. "I'm asking you, as tutor to my children, and recent resident of this old house, and as someone given the highest recommendations in the land for her skill at education, and with the esteem of many others besides, to become my lawfully wedded wife!"

Should I have waited to give my answer? I think not. I was completely seduced, stunned, and grateful. With his dark hair combed off his brow, and his blue eyes that shone like marbles, and his strong physique, he looked like an Adonis. Taken aback by his hand upon my breast, but also thrilled with the prospect of being married to this generous, rich, and obviously romantic man, I suddenly assented.

"Of course," I said, "it would be my pleasure to be married to you and be the new mother to your children. This is all rather quick, but I'm honored to comply with your proposal. And if I'd known your feelings sooner, I might have flirted with you more!" I smiled and grasped his hand in mine. He got to his feet and clasped me again in his embrace, with a sigh that seemed to express the relief of a man who, as in archery, had been unsure of his mark but was now satisfied.

Then he kissed me again, and I nearly swooned with delight, and, dear Reader – it is now summer of the following year – we are today happily wed and with another child on the way.

To he who says, "Look before you leap," I answer, "She who hesitates is lost!" Two opposite pieces of advice, but for me the second was the best, the truest, and the most providential. I am very happy today in our lovely manor home, with my husband, our children, and my pleasant thoughts of our long future together. May the good Heavens bless everyone so.

RED DIRT COWBOY

ASH ORLANDO

The sun rose hot in Adam's eyes as he searched the horizon.

A wild Australian eagle rose from the furthest field and lifted through the sky, tracing gold through the air like a blessing.

This country, he thought, this country could bring me home anytime.

The tall gum trees above him brought welcome shade, their long limbs stretching. Currently a family of three white cockatoos roosted, their screeching cries and outlandish manners bringing in the day. They swung and played, shouting happily. Other farmers thought them a pest. One big flock could pull off the gutters on your house when bored, causing damage and wreaking havoc. But Adam adored them, especially when they travelled en masse in a huge white cloud, screeching. They were joy itself, set free.

Visitors at the Farm, and they were seldom, were always commenting on the quiet of the bush. But to Adam he heard everything, the wide river rushing down behind his home, the quiet contented murmuring of sheep, the caw of the big black ravens picking the meat from old bones near the road. It was alive with sound.

At night the possums had taken to running along the old

corrugated iron roof of his farmhouse, just at dusk. They were noisy too, but they came like clockwork. Just lately, he had welcomed it, the ruckus and the screeching. Living alone, and stuck only with the thoughts in his head, his mind turned his troubles over too many times. Financial worries, the concerns of distant family, the health of his livestock.

And always, always, like a painful bruise, his thoughts turned back to that old love, those many years ago. There was nothing he could do to keep those thoughts out.

Adam slouched casually on the fence line and ran his hands along the wooden timbers. He thought briefly of his own father, and his grandad before that, who had laid these timbers and kept the place neat. The wood was already warming under his touch, and the growing day.

It would be a hot one, he thought, and turned his thoughts to the tasks ahead. The neighbours' paddocks lay spread before him in different coloured crops, like tablecloths laid for a feast. His own sheep grazing peacefully nearby, in his fields.

He was a quiet man and had been a quiet boy. He had grown up alone with his Dad, just accepting what was in front of him.

Of late, Adam hadn't even kept up the roses or the old vegetable garden. He had no time. Since his Dad had passed six month prior, he had been here on his own, and preferred it. At different times he got farmhands in to help with the livestock, but right now he could manage on his own.

He didn't want to admit it, but he was lost without his father. They had grown up together, in a way, after his mother had run out and left them. He had built his identity around his father.

Adam's faded denim jeans fit his large frame comfortably, and his old boots were well worn in. He was a bigger man, broad across the shoulders. He took up space but wished he didn't, and when he was young he was sat at the back of every classroom so nobody could pay any attention. He listened, did his school work, and went home. Nothing special to anyone, but on the farm he had a light touch with the animals and he became known for it. People would come and ask for his help with a hurt lamb, or an angry sow. He could calm an animal, sense what was wrong. It was just something in his nature. Now that he was in his late twenties, and school far behind him, he could take his time and live life at the pace he liked.

It suited him, or it had, until his father passed. Now there was a restlessness in him he hadn't known was there.

Either way, there was work to be done before midday, and there was no-one here but Adam to do it.

With a sigh, he drew his work gloves from the back pocket of his faded jeans, swept the sweat from his brow, and made his way to the sheds. He tilted his akubra on his head and started walking.

Back in town, Jacob was at a loose end. He was at his mother's house. Having thrown down a breakfast of eggs and beans and bacon, he was loafing on the porch, scuffing his boots on the boards.

"You're bored already," said his mother, pushing open the screen door. "You could go help your Uncle at the shop, you know. He could use it."

Jacob scowled at the thought. He was raised without a father, and his Uncle had seen fit to school him every chance he got. Sometimes with fists but most often with words. A lot of that had happened at the shop, scattered auto parts everywhere. Grease on his uncle's fists and his overalls straining at the waist over time. His Uncle was like a local lord, throwing his power around every chance he could get.

It had made him bitter; he would admit. Filled with fury, he had taken it out on everybody he could. He got known around town as a bully, someone who would act in anger before a word had ever been uttered. Inside him a hollow feeling followed him wherever he went. He tried to drink his way through it but nothing worked.

"I'm okay Mama, I'm just gonna sit here awhile. Take in the town."

She snorted at that. His mother's house was on the mainstreet, but the town was tiny. Several shops were dotted along the road, but fewer now that the old highway was replaced by a bigger one down south. Not much traffic through now. Even the old freight trucks went the easier way.

He remembers the day clearly that his mother closed her hair salon and sold her stock to a woman in another town. Even the chairs she sold on, everything. She went home with nothing and closed her door shut against the summer winds.

The next day Jacob, at the age of 22, had set out for the city for work.

He had thrown his clothes and a few old things into a duffle bag and hitched out of town. He had found work easy enough on one of the bigger farms. He was good with horses, so. He could work anywhere really. The work was seasonal but enough. He sent enough money home for his mother and kid sister so they would never go without.

He was proud to do that. He was proud to keep on doing it too, but once in a while he drifted home to see her, see she was okay, and drifted off again. He had only been home three times in ten years though. That was enough for him. Something about being at home shot him through with loneliness, anyways. It was good to stay moving.

He eyed the truck in the driveway out front. It was red, which he loved. He knew it was vanity to buy a red car, but at the age of 17 he had started saving every cent to get it. Worked mornings and nights after school. When he was eighteen, he went to the Stock Show & Rodeo out west and came home with his hands on the steering wheel. It was his pride and joy. He had seen it, knew he paid too much for it, but had to have it.

It was a 1996 Ford F-250 XLT with a Power Stroke diesel. It was old, but it was beautiful, and most importantly it was his.

In a moment of pure sacrifice, when he had left for the city all those years ago, Jacob had left his mother the truck. At least he could know for sure his uncle would take care of it, keep the engine smooth and do tires for free. At least he could be sure of that. She needed to get around town, he knew. What if something happened and baby Daisy needed to get to the hospital? Anything could happen.

It was never clear who was the Daddy of baby Daisy, reflected Jacob. Some out of towner he guessed. It didn't really matter to him. Family is family. Blood is blood. He would take care of his own.

"You're making me anxious, just sitting there," said his mother. "Get out and go for a drive would you. Give your mother some peace."

He started at that, seeing as he was nothing but quiet, but smiled when he saw she was joking. She adored for him to be home. Fussed over him for something foolish, baking cakes and roast dinners. Anything he wanted. She never said much, but he ate like a king, and told her so.

He nodded at her, lifted his hat down from the hook. With one movement he took the keys from the post and walked towards the truck.

He could not disguise the eagerness in his step as he creaked open the old truck door and slid in.

Ah, he thought. Coming home is good.

He drove the main street fast, faster than he needed to, just to feel the engine buck and roar to life. His Uncle had kept it well. The old leather seats groaned a little as he shifted gear, keeping his eyes on the road. Finally, he had it in fifth gear as he sped down open roads, field after field falling behind him. He could have shouted for the pleasure of it. The clean open air through the windows, his arm leaning out, the sun beating down. Nothing more to anything in life but this.

The whole time he pretended he might not go. The whole time he just drove, in what might look like aimless circles to others, but became a certain steady path. He was going to the Macklin farm, down by the river. He couldn't help it. He needed to see Adam.

His heart took to thumping in his chest, like it was twice its size. Sweat on his brow, he gripped the steering wheel with an iron grasp.

Time had passed, he knew. But it might be months until he was here again. And he just had to know. He told himself, it wouldn't matter either way.

But his body betrayed him, and the old yearning kicked back in like it had never left.

The old truck was running smooth, and the road unfurled like a ribbon.

Jacob was lost in his thoughts when he saw it – a dark shape on the side of the road. He immediately veered the truck off to the side of the road and ran to check.

A gorgeous red-tailed black cockatoo lay to one side, moving but only a little. Rarer than its cousin the white cockatoo, the black cockatoo was shy and often could be seen but not heard. It had a distinctive call, but mostly stayed clear of people altogether. When it flew, its scarlet feathers were like a fan of wildfire through the sky. It was a beautiful bird.

Internally, Jacob cursed. Some bastard had hit it and kept going.

It was stunned but he couldn't see blood. It might be okay, but he needed to get it somewhere dark and cool so it could recover. The possibility otherwise if it didn't recover – he couldn't think about it. All his life, Jacob had hated to see animals suffer. He had stayed clear of cattle farming and livestock altogether, preferring to work with crops.

At his old job, he had once seen a lame horse shot dead. Unlike the other men, he had turned his head at the last moment to stare at the ground, his heart feeling hot. It was right to do, to take the life of the horse. Seeing the injury of the horse after a bad fall, the farmer knew it, and knew the beast would never recover. Still the farmer talked gently to the animal, in a quiet voice Jacob couldn't hear. When the shot rang out, it fell dead in a sudden movement, hitting the ground heavily. It had shocked Jacob, the noise. Not the gunshot. But the sound of the beast falling.

But its suffering was done, and that was right. Didn't mean Jacob would ever get used to it.

He wrapped the huge bird in his old flannelette shirt from the backseat. It didn't move much, which was a bad sign. He gently placed her on the passenger seat, alarmed by her quietness.

He started to drive.

. . .

Adam heard the truck before he saw it and stopped his work, wondering.

He started walking up to the old house, seeing dirt from the truck filling the air as it came down the long driveway, too fast. It roared to a halt, and he saw with a shock that it was Jacob behind the wheel.

In an instant his blood ran hot, and then cold, then hot again.

This could not be happening.

Jacob flew from the driver's seat, and came towards him, his lean body agitated and raw.

"Adam," started Jacob, "It wasn't me that hit her, but I got her now. Take a look, can you?"

He turned before Adam could say a word and went straight to the other side of the truck. Lifting the bird out, he cradled it in his arms.

"It's a red-tail," said Jacob, his eyes wide. "Gotta get her somewhere quiet and dark."

Without a word, Adam nodded and moved towards the farmhouse quickly. He pulled a large cardboard box out from the garden shed as he walked. He took the bird from Jacob and cradled her with one arm, like a child.

In the cool lounge room, he set the box down and got it ready. Gently, carefully, he took the cockatoo and unwrapped her. She struggled in his arms, panicked by the light. She cried out in alarm, twisting her body.

"Help me," said Adam, "I have to open her wings. See if they're broken."

Jacob complied and pulled the bird close to his chest. She raked at him, leaving swift and bloody claw marks beneath his singlet. He barely felt it but held her steady as Adam did what he could.

"Put her in the box, give her some rest. Maybe she'll be okay, maybe not. Wings seem intact. Might be internal bleeding. Won't know for a while." Adam held the box open as Jacob lowered her in.

Adam closed the box firmly, and the great bird stilled, comforted by the darkness.

"Take your shirt off," The instruction from Adam made Jacob's face instantly burn.

"What?"

"I need to see those scratches. Wait here."

Adam disappeared into the kitchen. He searched for the old first aid kit – it used to be… where was it? Maybe on top of the fridge? Okay got it.

When he got back to the room Jacob had pulled his singlet free, and three bloody lines were along his chest. His naked chest was golden in the bright midday light streaming through the tall windows.

Adam broke out in a sweat to see it.

"Adam, it doesn't hurt," Jacob started. "I don't really need—"

"Hold still." Adam pulled open the kit and started rifling through.

"It's fine. Look. It's nothing."

Adam stood and came towards him. At the last moment he reached instead for Jacob's cheek and with a rough hand traced along his jawline, with gentleness.

"It's been years," Adam said. "I thought maybe you'd—"

"I had things to do," Jacob twisted and moved back. "Plus, I heard about you and Emma. All them wedding bells in the air."

Adam laughed, then saw he was serious. "Me and Emma. Well. That was, just – like a high school thing. But you and me—"

"You and me? There's no you and me."

"Emma didn't know me, Jacob. Didn't know about – well, this." Adam stood, looking down.

"And what is this," said Jacob, almost shouting. "What the hell is this?"

"I don't know. I've been trying to figure it out for years. You've been gone years. I still don't know."

"You do know." Jacob went to him then, his lean figure moving closer to Adam. "I can tell you know."

Jacob kissed him then, hungrily, pushing his hand through Adam's hair to draw him in.

From inside Adam a deep groan came, a groan of longing and need and all the sleepless nights of staring at the ceiling, all the days of his body yearning for release and real comfort.

He had loved Emma, it was true. But not with this passion, not the way it was with Jacob. Nothing was this way. He couldn't deny it.

Adam grabbed Jacob's waist, pulled him close. Their heavy belt buckles clashed, the soft feeling of denim against denim sparking them both to life. Jacob smelled the way he always did, like engine oil and sweat. It went straight to Adam's head, and he inhaled it, remembering every other time they had stolen time together.

Nights under the stars, in the back of Jacob's truck. Scuffling boots, wrestling and almost fighting each other to see who could claim the prize of who was on top. Both men laughing. Adam's bigger size almost always winning out, with Jacob's quickness claiming his share of victory. They had been safe there, in the empty paddocks under broad night skies. Nobody had known. At school, they had avoided each other completely, to protect themselves.

But nights when they could, they would light up each other's bodies like miracles. Like a holy truth, the way it made them feel. Real and honest and good.

They fell together now with all the memories of those times. Adam pushed Jacob onto the lounge, putting his strength and need behind it. They kissed again, and Jacob bit his lip playfully.

Adam threw his strong arms around Jacob, the leather lounge creaking softly. He embraced him completely, with ownership and certainty. Jacob lay his head on Adam's heart, like they used to do under starlight. Their hearts echoed a rhythm between them of raw pleasure.

Adam ran his hands down Jacob's naked back, feeling his skin, the span of his shoulders. The familiar shape of his body. He pulled Jacob up and began kissing him some more, feeling his need strengthen. It had been a long time, too long.

Jacob's body answered his need and Adam's breath quickened.

He could feel the hot urgency of what was happening. He started to grind a little, testing Jacob's limits. Could it really be just like it was? Just as simple, just as good?

Suddenly a high call came, shocking them both. It was the cockatoo, clawing at the box. She cried again, this time more fiercely.

Jacob moved to the box, and between the two of them they lifted it outside, past the porch and to the driveway. The bird scrambled frantically inside.

"Well let's just see I guess," murmured Adam, as his hands pulled open the box to look. "Maybe it was that she was just stunned."

But the bird knew her mind already. With a last cry, the red-tail cockatoo pushed free of the box and lifted into the air, straight out into the open sky. She flew. Her open wings moved easily, cutting a shape of freedom across the blue. She was fine. She was magic.

"She's gone," breathed Jacob with relief, one hand shielding his eyes from the sun as he gazed after her trail in the air.

"But you. You're staying," said Adam, and pulled him inside the farmhouse.

The broken fence be damned. His hands had better things to do.

Jacob was home and it was time to get to work.

LE PAIN DE L'AMORE

NICHOLE BLAKE

"So I said to him, get your hands off me! And lose my number! Whatever happened to romance anyway?" Erin stabbed a piece of lettuce and poked it in her mouth.

We were having lunch at *Bonne Nourriture*, a trendy new French bistro that just opened up downtown. The menu, black with a simple white signature font, boasted locally sourced meats, organically grown produce and artisan breads. I was stuffing my face with one such artisan bread, a golden sourdough roll with the perfect ratio of crusty, chewy exterior to fluffy, light interior, while Erin, my best friend, ranted about her most recent manscapade.

"Is it too much for a girl to want a little romance before the wam-bam? Kat? Hello? Kat?" Erin waved her hand in front of my face.

"What? Sorry, yes, mmm." I said between bites. "Oh my god, Erin, you have to try this bread, it's better than sex." I spread a thick layer of soft butter across another piece and stuffed it in my mouth.

Erin frowned. "You really need to get laid."

She wasn't wrong. It had been eight months since Jarrid and I broke up, eight months since I'd caught him in bed with the girl who lived in the apartment above his, and eight months of drowning my sorrows in whatever carbs I could get my hands on at any given moment. Pizza, pasta, doughnuts, french fries, I didn't discriminate. Since the break-up I'd gained 10 pounds, and if I didn't put an end to the eating frenzy soon, twenty was not far off.

"I know, I know. I just… haven't been feeling it. The idea of getting back out there. Ugh. Jarrid and I were together for five years. We were supposed to be getting married, you know… and I… I…" I could feel my throat tightening up.

"Jarrid's a wanker. He's always been a wanker, and I always said you deserved better. It's time Kat. It's time for you to get back out there."

Back. Out. There. The dating world. It may as well have been outer space. The idea terrified me.

"I'd have no idea where to even look."

"Well, no one's going to just fall on your doorstep, if that's what you're thinking. I look every morning and it hasn't happened yet. You should try online. That's where I meet all my dates."

"And look how well that's worked out for you." I shoved another piece of bread into my mouth. "I just really want to meet someone, you know, organically."

"Kat, you're picking a man, not a melon."

"I know, it's just that, when I meet someone, I want it to be special. I want to be one of those couples that has a great how-they-met-story. Something our children will roll their eyes at, and can recite word for word because they've heard it so many times. And they'll tell their children, and our grandchildren will know the story of how Nana met Papa, and that happily ever after really is possible. I thought I had that with Jarrid. We had a great story."

"A great story doesn't end with your fiance cheating on you. Jarrid was not your happily ever after, and there's nothing wrong with a little happiness right now, even if it's not ever-after."

"They say it happens when you're not looking for it," I told her.

"Well then, don't look for it. Look for something else. Just keep an open mind. Try something new. Have some fun. There are dating sites for whatever you're into. You've heard of Match, EHarmony, Tinder – but if none of those tickles your pickle, there's also Sugardaddy.com. Or, what about Cougar.com? Fancy yourself with a younger man?"

"I'm only 28."

"I'm sure there's a hot 21-year-old out there who would just love to butter your muffin."

"Ok. Nevermind about my muffin. I get your point. I'll get out there."

Erin offered to drop me off at my apartment, but I decided to walk instead. If I was going to get back into the dating scene, I'd need to lose the break-up weight, or at the very least not gain any more. No more drowning my sorrows in carbs. What I needed was salads, salads, and more salads. I'd make a quick detour to the store to pick up some fresh veggies. This wasn't my neighborhood, but I thought I remembered a little mom and pop grocery just a few blocks away.

After wandering around and circling back a few times, it was obvious I was lost. I pulled out my phone to look for directions when I noticed a sign on the front of a red brick building. It read *"Le Pain de L'Amour"* and had a logo of a fat cherub with wings, but instead of shooting an arrow, it was shooting a baguette into an oversized red heart. I'd seen the same logo on the back of the *Bonne Nourriture* menu where it listed the names of the businesses it had locally sourced from. This was where they got the better-than-sex bread!

This was a sign, I was sure of it. This was the Gods telling me that my carb-loading pity party wasn't over just yet. This was not the time for salads, or for online dating, or for dating of any kind. Erin wouldn't be happy, but I wasn't ready. I'd get out there in my own time. And who needed men when better-than-sex bread existed? I'd pop in and buy a couple of loaves before heading home.

A small gated courtyard full of overgrown trees, untrimmed shrubbery, and half-dead begonias surrounded the building, and a couple of strings of outdoor lights dangled from a branch, as if someone had abandoned the project midway. The iron gate groaned softly as I pushed it open. I walked up the steps to the entrance, pulled open the front door, and stepped inside.

A weak stream of sunlight filtered through the heavy drapes that partially covered the windows. The walls, like the outside of the building, were worn red brick, and the floor was dark polished wood. Exposed pipes ran across the top of the open pitched ceiling, and at the rear of the darkened room stood two enormous stone fireplaces. No, not fireplaces – ovens. Stacked next to them, a grouping of large, flat shovel-like paddles of varying shapes and sizes leaned against the wall. On the left side of the room stood three metal shelving units filled with numerous bowls and baskets, also in varying shapes and sizes, each covered with a thin cloth. On the right side of the room were more metal shelving units full of cooked loaves – boules, baguettes and other shapes of breads I didn't know the names of. In the middle of the room was an enormous carved wooden table, and standing next to it, the most beautiful man I'd ever seen.

He was tall, six feet at least, and had a slightly thin yet muscular build. His dark hair was pulled back into a short ponytail at the nape of his neck, and his face had the outline of what looked to be the beginnings of a short beard, dark like his hair.

"Salut, how are you?" he said with an accent. French, of course. What else? "I'm Michael. Are you here for the position?"

"The position?" I asked. I mean, I could think of a few I'd be up for.

"Oui, the position for the assistante? The ad posted in the journal… ah… newspaper, this morning?"

I didn't need a translator to tell me what assistante meant. Did people still post jobs in the newspaper anymore? Well, I guess hot French guys did. But did anyone actually *look* for jobs in the newspaper anymore? I didn't think so, which meant he probably wouldn't get a lot of applicants, which meant that…

"Yes, I am. Here. For the positions." I blushed. "I mean position. Assistant position. That's exactly the reason I'm here." The words jumped out of my mouth before I could stop them. I didn't need a job, I already had a job. Not one I especially liked, but who liked their job? The pay wasn't great, and I hated my boss, and I also had a crap ton of unused vacation time and possibly an imaginary sick grandmother who lived out of state and needed extended care.

"Ah, *bien*. You are the first one."

And hopefully, the only one.

He dusted his hands off on the front of the white canvas apron that was tied around his waist and walked over to me, extending his hand forward.

"And you are?"

"Oh, yes, sorry." I smiled sheepishly. "I'm Kat. Katherine, actually, but everyone calls me Kat. You can too, if you like. Kat. Or Katherine. Or Kat. Whatever you want to call me. You're fine. I mean it's fine." I reached out and placed my hand in his, and he held it there, suspended in the air for what seemed like a full minute, not quite shaking it, but not letting go either.

His eyes were the lightest color of brown, with flecks of gold. *Cognac mixed with honey*, I thought. He smiled a slightly crooked smile, and my heart jumped a little in my chest, and I felt a heat rise to my cheeks. I looked away quickly.

"Hmmm… well if it is my choice I don't think I will call you Katherine or Kat. I will call you *Minette*, which in French means kitten. What do you think?"

It could mean frog face for all I cared. As long as he said it with those lips and that accent. I nodded and smiled stupidly.

"So tell me, *Minette*, do you have any experience with artisan bread making?"

"Well, no, not exactly. But when I was little, during holiday dinners, I would always help my Grandmother, *moi Grand-mere*… make the dinner rolls." Who knew those two years of high school French would come in handy someday?

"Ah, the American dinner rolls." He frowned. "I am familiar. Well, that is not the kind of bread we make here. All the bread here is naturally leavened. Do you know what that means?"

"I think so," I said, remembering a field trip in the 6th grade to the San Francisco Sourdough Company. "You use a starter, right?"

"*Oui*, a starter, but in French we call it a *poolish*. Come, I'll show you."

Again he took my hand in his, and I felt the warmth of it spread up my arm and throughout my body. He led me through the main room, past the ovens, through a narrow door to a smallish kitchen. Two large industrial size refrigerators stood against one wall, and next to them, a double stainless steel sink, with a large drainboard and pull out faucet. Next to that, ceiling to floor shelving held various bins, crocks and canisters.

Michael pulled a large glass container from a shelf and set it on the small wooden island in the center of the room. He opened the lid to reveal a thick bubbling batter-like substance that had a pungent though not unpleasant yeasty smell.

"This is the *poolish*, or as you call it, the starter. It was handed down to me by my *Grandmere*, and to her by her *Grandmere*. It has been in my family for *beaucoup generations*. We use this to make the levain, which is what creates the magic bubbles that will make the bread rise."

He spooned a large portion of the *poolish* into a bowl and sat it on a scale, and then added an equal amount of water and flour, and mixed them together to form another batter, slightly thicker than the first.

"Now we wait for the levain to double in size. Can you tell when something has doubled in size?" He raised an eyebrow and smiled that crooked smile. Was he flirting? He stood so close, I could smell him, a heady, slightly spicy smell. I felt blood rising to my cheeks again, and… other places. I reached for the side of the table to steady myself.

"Hello? Hello?" A woman's voice called from the other room. "Is anyone here? I'm here about the assistant bread baker's position."

Michael walked over to the doorway, turning back to look at me once again, then leaned out and said, "Apologies, but the position has already been filled."

∼

LE PAIN DE L'AMORE

It wasn't really work. I was on vacation after all, and I'd be lying if I said it wasn't the best one I'd ever had. Micheal was a patient, caring, hot, teacher. Did I mention he was hot? Sometimes I'd pretend I didn't understand something just so he'd explain it again, this time a little slower, a little closer. I could listen to that voice, that accent forever, and his scent, a mix of sandalwood soap, his own light perspiration, and the freshly baked smell of the boulangerie, was intoxicating. I'd never believed in pheromones before, but now I was a believer.

I loved hearing Micheal laugh, and I loved it best when I was the reason for it. One time, trying to reach a small bag of pastry flour perched on the edge of the top shelf, I'd made a make-shift step stool out of an empty flour bin. Standing on it tip-toe, I stretched slightly forward, trying to close the last few inches I needed to reach the bag. The flour bin slipped out from under me and I grabbed a hold of the bag of pastry flour, thinking it would somehow steady me. It did not. I tumbled to the ground, pulling the bag of pastry flour down on top of me. It had not been closed properly, and a puff of fine white power exploded into the air, falling onto my head and all over my face. Micheal ran to me, asking if I was hurt, and I shook my head no, blinking white powder out of my eyes. Then we both burst out laughing.

The next morning, when I arrived at work, Micheal greeted me at the door, his face covered in white flour. "This part of our new uniform now, no?" And we began laughing all over again.

After I'd mastered the skill of the poolish and the levain, Micheal taught me about autolyse – the rest period required after the initial mixing of water, flour and salt, before incorporating the levain. Many bakers skipped this step, he said, but it was essential for a strong gluten structure, and it should not be rushed. Only time and patience would produce a superior product, and so I applied this theory to myself as well. Even though I wanted to be doing more than just baking bread with Micheal, I also wanted the strong structure and superior product that only time and patience would produce. So, I put myself on autolyse, and I waited.

The bulk of the baking was done early in the morning, so the bread would be ready for delivery by the time the truck arrived. This also allowed the ovens to cool down before the midday heat turned the old brick building into an oven itself.

Bright and early each morning, Micheal would preheat the ovens while I began mixing the poolish that we would use to create the levain for the loaves we would create that day. Micheal would bake the loaves that he had shaped the day before and had proofed overnight. I would mix the flours, different types depending on what flavor of bread we were making, with water and salt, then leave the vats of dough to autolyse. Then, I would package the semi-cooled loaves into crisp brown bags, closing each with a sticker bearing the *Le Pain de L'Amore* logo. While Micheal finished baking, I would clean up, take inventory, and order any supplies that needed restocking. Then Michael would shape the new loaves to be baked the following day.

The weeks passed quickly, and I kept extending my leave at work. My nana was still very, very ill. No, I didn't know when I'd be coming back. I'd used up all my vacation time and was now out on what my job considered an unpaid personal leave of absence. Since I was no longer receiving a paycheck from them, I'd been supplementing my bakery income with the money I'd saved for my wedding. They wouldn't hold my job forever, and my savings wouldn't last forever either.

"So what's happening with Mr. French-Bread-PonyTail man?" Erin grinned at me and took a sip of her latte. Micheal had asked me to stop by *Bonne Nourriture* to pick up a check for a large order, and I'd asked Erin to meet me for coffee.

"Don't call him that. His name is Micheal. And it's not one of those creepy, old, hippy guy kind of ponytails. It's the hot, French guy kind of ponytail."

"I didn't know there was a difference."

"Well, there is."

"Does he ever wear a man-bun?"

"Oh God no."

"Well. At least there's that. And he calls you Minnie? Like Minnie Mouse?"

"No, Minette. It means kitten in French."

"Rawr." Erin clawed at the air. "Tell me. Is it true what they say about a man with big boules?"

"What's that?" I played along, already knowing the answer.

"That he has a really, really, big baguette?"

I laughed. "I don't know anything about his baguette. We haven't gone there yet."

"Well, why the hell not? What are you waiting for?"

"I'm waiting for him to make the first move. And he hasn't. And with us working together, I'm not sure how that would go."

"You know that's not your real job, right?"

"I wish it was. The thought of going back to my stuffy cubicle, working eight-to-five, shuffling papers all day, depresses me. There's something really satisfying about working at the bakery, and it's not just about seeing Micheal every day. I actually enjoy the work."

"So, what are you going to do? It's not like you can afford to quit your job and work exclusively for Micheal. You could ask him for a raise, but that probably might be a little weird if you two were to… you know."

"Yeah. I know."

"So what are you going to do?"

I shrugged. "I guess I'll have to quit."

By the time I arrived at the bakery, Micheal had already been there for hours. *Bonne Nourriture* also did catering, and someone had placed an order for 100 baguettes that needed to be ready for delivery first thing the next morning. Today would not be business as usual, and instead of only baking in the morning, the ovens would go full steam all day.

I busied myself with the work and tried to not think about quitting, about having to go back to a job I hated, and about leaving Micheal, but it was no use. Every time I looked at him, my eyes filled with tears. Once he caught me brushing them away. I told him it was just the heat from the ovens making them burn, and he insisted I go outside to take a break.

When we'd finally packaged the last baguette and put it in the box, ready for the delivery trucks in the morning, I was exhausted, not just physically, but emotionally. I was determined to tell him that night and get it over with. It wouldn't be any easier tomorrow. I was in the small kitchen, trying to work up my nerve when Micheal called to me from the main room.

"Minette, aren't you hungry?" He asked. "We haven't eaten all day."

Micheal pulled out a small portion of dough from underneath the counter. He sprinkled a generous portion of flour on the large table, then using his hands he stretched and flattened the dough into a thin circular disc. He disappeared into the kitchen, and a few minutes later returned with a bowl containing several round balls of fresh mozzarella, a small tin of imported tomatoes, a few cloves of garlic, and a sprig of fresh basil.

"I didn't know French people knew how to make pizza," I said.

"French people know how to make everything," He smiled. "But I also have a great uncle who is Italian, and he taught me about making pizza."

He opened the tin of tomatoes, chopped them roughly, and, using the flat side of a knife, he crushed the garlic, chopped it with the basil, and added both to the tomatoes before spreading the mixture over the circle of dough. He sliced the mozzarella into coin shaped pieces, layered them on top, then slid the whole thing into the last remaining lit oven.

"Why don't we eat outside?" Micheal said, handing me a bottle of wine and two glasses that he took from the cabinet.

LE PAIN DE L'AMORE

"Outside?" I asked. As far as I knew, there was nowhere to eat outside.

"Yes, outside." He motioned towards the front door. I took the wine and glasses from him and walked out into the courtyard, not sure what I would find, but under one of the trees I saw a small iron bistro table and two folding chairs. I poured each of us a glass and set the bottle on the table just as a light came on overhead. I looked up, remembering the string of lights I'd seen hanging from the branches that first day. Sounds of light jazz floated up from the nightclub at the end of the block.

Micheal arrived with the pizza. It was hot and golden and bubbly, and smelled delicious, and, despite the knot in my stomach, I was starving.

"You deserved something special after all of your hard work today. I wanted you to know I could never have managed this day, or any of days before it, without you. A votre sante." Micheal said, raising his glass to mine.

I clinked my glass against his.

"Micheal, there's something I need to tell you,"

"What is that *Minette?*"

"I… I… I'm starving."

"Well then, let us eat!"

The pizza was divine, and I told Micheal so.

"The secret is the crust. Instead of traditional kneading, I use a stretch and fold method that my great uncle taught me. It allows for the flavor of the dough to fully develop. And tomatoes from Italy don't hurt. Before I opened the boulangerie, I considered opening a pizzeria instead."

"You what?" I asked, stopping mid-bite.

"I considered opening a pizzeria instead."

I looked around the courtyard, at the overgrown trees with the strings of lights hanging haphazardly from the branches, the wilting flowers, the smell of fresh baked bread , the jazz music, and something clicked.

"Well, why don't you? Why don't we?"

"Why don't we what?"

"Open a pizzeria. This place would be perfect. We could trim the trees, plant some flowers, and string more lights. It would take a little money, but I have a small savings, and we could get a business loan for the rest. We could do it together."

Michael looked at me, not saying anything, and I realized I was talking too fast, too loud.

"We could be business partners," I said, lowering my voice.

"You want to be business partners?" He frowned. He seemed less than pleased.

After that, the conversation grew awkward, and stilted. I left shortly after, telling him it had been a long day and I'd see him in the morning.

The next morning Micheal was quiet, and he seemed to be making a concentrated effort to be anywhere I wasn't. When I went into the small kitchen, he immediately found something to do in the main room, and when I went into the main room, he immediately found something to do in the kitchen.

Finally, after going into the kitchen once more just to have him find a reason to leave again, I decided I couldn't take it anymore. I'd have to take a chance and tell him how I truly felt. If it meant losing him, getting fired and having to go back to my old job, so be it. It was a risk I'd have to take. But I needed to see that smile on his face one more time. I knew what I had to do.

I pulled the bag of pastry flour down from the top shelf, stood over the sink, held the bag over my face, closed my eyes, and gave it a squeeze. A plume of fine white powder exploded from the bag and onto my face.

"Micheal," I said, as I walked back to the main room. "We need to talk."

"Yes, we do." He stood at the table with back to me.

"I know I said I wanted to be business partners, and I do. But that's not all of it. Truth is, I want us to be more than that. These last months have been both amazing and torturous for me. I think about you from the time I wake up in the morning, until the time I go to bed each night, and I look forward to coming to work every day, because I get to spend it with you. So, you need to know, before you make your decision, I could never be just a business partner, because I feel so much more for you than that."

He turned around slowly and looked at me as I blinked white powder out of my eyes with the most serious dead-pan face I could muster. And then he gave me the one thing I so desperately needed to see at the moment – that crooked smile. He shook his head, laughing. He picked up a towel off the table and came over to me, tilted my chin up with one hand, and with the other, wiped the flour from my face.

"If we are going to be business partners, you'll need to learn the special technique to make the crust. Let me show you how."

He led me back to the table, pulled a small amount of wet dough from the plastic proofing tub onto the surface of the table. With one hand he grabbed a corner of the dough, then pulled it up over the opposite side. He gave the dough a quarter turn and repeated the movement.

"Here, you try." He placed his hands on my shoulders and steered me toward the table, and that familiar warmth spread from his hands through my body, as it did every time he touched me.

I grabbed the dough with one one hand and purposely only stretched it halfway, knowing I was doing it wrong. Then I did it wrong again.

"No, not like that," he said.

"Show me."

He moved behind me, his arm on either side of me and his face right above my right shoulder, his breath on my neck. He took my hands in his and pushed them into the wet dough.

"Like this," he said, using one of my hands to grab the corner of the sticky dough, pulling it up and over to the opposite side. He gave the dough a quarter turn and did it again. "Slowly. And again. Again. Can you feel the tension developing, *Minette*?"

"Yes." I whispered. I could feel a lot more developing than just the tension in the dough.

"The benefit to a slow stretch and fold is an increase in volume. It also helps to create an open, airy, interior crumb." His lips grazed my ear.

"Mmmmhmmm." My mouth no longer seemed capable of actual words.

"Here, you try." His hands left mine, and he wrapped his arms tightly around my waist, and pulled me closer. I continued turning the dough, pulling one corner of it over the other, as he began to kiss my neck.

As his kisses became stronger and more insistent, I realized we were no longer just making bread, but something else entirely. I turned and met his mouth with mine.

"When the dough is finally ready to bake," Michael whispered. "It will be billowy and soft." Which described exactly how I felt at that moment.

"If baked too early, it will not rise to its fullest potential." His hands traveled to places that had not been touched in a long time, and I definitely felt he was about to reach my fullest potential.

"If baked too late, the dough will over-ferment and collapse." He lifted me up onto the table, sliding my dress up over my hips, and pulled me toward him.

"The oven must be preheated to the highest temperature, and the baking vessel must be very hot as well." My oven was as hot as it was going to get, and so was his baking vessel… if that's what you wanted to call it. And at that moment, I did.

"The final burst of steam just after the loaf is put into the hot oven is known as oven spring."

And like that, I was sprung. Or as the French called it – *la petite mort!*

I had to admit Erin was right. This was so much better than the bread. And it was a great story.

ENOUGH TO KILL

JIM TRITTEN AND SANDI HOOVER

A gleaming full moon illuminated the light blue MINI Cooper. A couple nuzzled close together, their heads barely rising above the black convertible top. The woman's hair waved in the gentle breeze coming up the Hollywood hills to this lovers' lane overlook.

The man pulled back so he could hold his lover's gaze. He caressed her cheek. "Honey, I can't wait until next month."

The woman pulled him back to her, kissed him hard, and nuzzled close to his ear. "We don't have to wait until next month, silly."

Their heads bobbed from side to side in a passionate clinch. The woman broke free, sat up in her seat, and faced him. She unbuttoned her blouse and reached toward the man.

"And cut," the *Hawks Landing* director shouted. "Good work, you two. Everybody — that's a wrap."

Nick and Grace exchanged perfunctory smiles as they did every time they kissed for the cameras.

Grace put on her top, punched Nick in the arm, and said, "You're really enjoying this, aren't you?"

He winked, smiled again as they strolled toward the exit. "I'm headed home. How about you?"

"I've gotta change first, kiss my darling Tim, grab Jimmie, and head on to Little League practice. Hey, when are we gonna work again?"

"Tuesday, I think. Enjoy the weekend. Give Tim a 'hey' and the kid a hug from me."

"Same to Megan and Josh."

Nick walked out the exit to the parking lot while Grace skipped to her trailer humming the *Hawks Landing* theme song.

∽

Nick throttled his Ford F-150 Platinum toward Laurel Canyon Boulevard. A photo of Grace lit the touchscreen display, and he toggled his steering wheel switch to answer the incoming call.

"Nick, we've gotta talk...."

Silence lingered. *Goddammit, what did I do now?*

"No, sweetheart, this is not about us."

He exhaled. "OK, you had me going there. Talk quickly; I'm almost in the canyon."

"Someone left a note in my trailer."

"What did it say?"

She whispered, "It says — 'I know what happened ten years ago.'"

Nick's hands tensed on the steering wheel. All he heard was the rumble of the engine, and the whoosh of traffic headed south on the other side of the road.

Grace blurted, "What am I gonna do?"

"You mean what are *we* going to do? Go to practice and then home like nothing's happened. Bring the note to the Little League game tomorrow morning. You can come without Tim, right?"

"Yeah, he'll welcome sleeping in. See you at third base."

Nick pushed the toggle switch. *The Twins will have their work cut for them. Here we go again. Just when we thought we were out.*

∽

The wooden bleachers creaked as Nick walked up the empty stands near third base. Grace was sitting alone on the top row, running shoes on the lower level and a Dodgers' cap pulled down to shade her eyes from the sun. The smell of newly mown grass lingered in the warm morning air. "Where was it?" he asked, sitting down beside her.

"On my vanity table... held down by our 100th episode award."

"Any hint who sent it?"

"No. Here, take a look." Grace handed him a plain, white envelope. "Wait, Jimmie's up to bat. Give me a sec."

Nick extracted the single sheet of white stationery and read in silence. All the note said was, "I know what happened ten years ago." Nick tilted the sheet up toward the sun and looked for indentations. It looked as if it had been printed from a computer and not typed. He replaced the note and tucked the envelope in his shirt pocket. He lifted his ball cap, squinted into the sun, and rubbed his hands over his face. *What are we going to do?*

Nick sighed, "Well, it gets its point across fast. Not like there's a lot of doubt what it means."

Grace viewed the playing field and shouted, "Come on, Jimmie, you can hit it." She turned to Nick and said in a lower voice, "Who'd a thunk I'd love being a stepmom... I thought no one saw what happened. The press reported the rebel forces killed him."

"What's prompted this? No one has cared about what occurred in Sirte in ten years. More fallout from Benghazi?"

"I don't care why! I'm a mother with a family I love. You know I quit because the Company demanded more than I could stomach. For God's sake, Nick, we've got to figure this out." Grace dropped her head down, hair swinging forward to cover her cheeks. Her breathing shuddered.

"Tell me what I don't know. Dammit." Feeling sympathetic, he reached his hand over to lightly rub Grace's back and shoulder.

Grace reached up and patted the top of his hand.

Nick thought *that's nice, but not like the old days.*

"I had no idea how different our lives would become when we married Tim and Megan."

"You know we had to do that."

Grace nodded, "Yep, it worked, but did you expect to fall in love?"

"Megan has become the love of my life."

"And here we are — I'm missing Tim, and we're watching our stepkids."

Nick squeezed her hand. *Aren't we both ready to end this affair?* "Hey, ump! You blind? That was way outside!" He returned to the reason they were sitting together. Libya. Ten years ago. They had shared a suite in the Mahari Hotel in Sirte… probably rubble now or occupied by U.S. Special Forces. "This time, we can't get backup or use the movie as cover. Regardless of the situation, our alter egos, the Twins, need to re-appear. We can't give in to blackmail."

Grace pulled her hand away and turned to Nick, "Maybe we should tell Langley?" She took out a tissue and wiped her face.

Nick grunted, laced his fingers behind his head, and leaned back. "No, we can't. They don't want anything to do with us. Who could have found out what we were doing in Libya in our spare time… that is unless this is all about how crazy you got when we were fooling around under the sheets?"

Grace winced. "Ha! I'm sure this isn't about a little recreational sex." She looked up and dazzled him with her Emmy Award-winning smile. She dropped her smile and became serious. "Our orders were to complete the mission *before* the capture — so he'd be assumed to be another casualty. When we eliminated him after capture, we crossed a line. Under international law, we're still liable for prosecution at The Hague."

"Wouldn't it be just like the Director to throw us under the bus to show the rest of the world the U.S. doesn't tolerate criminality?" Nick yelled out to the ballfield, "Good catch, Josh. Way to go."

Covered by the cheering, he faced Grace and said between clenched teeth, "Tell me how someone found out what we did and why in the hell are they coming after us now and not going to the press?" He took in a deep bushel of warm air and snorted out through his nose.

Their silence was punctuated by the sounds of "Batter up,"

"Striiike," and "Ball," only broken by the occasional crack of the bat meeting leather and other parents cheering. Two innings passed as the sun neared its zenith, and the breeze dropped to a wistful memory.

Grace slapped her knee, "You know; Aleksander Noli had a small part in *Assassin's Vendetta*. His scenes were shot in Libya." She rubbed her chin with a forefinger. "He made a big point of saying 'hi' the other day at a Screen Actor's Guild meeting."

"Now that you mention it, I ran into him at the commissary. He asked me if I could help him get a part on *Hawks Landing*."

"Whaddya tell him?"

Nick squirmed and said with a regretful tone, "Well, perhaps I was a bit less than sympathetic. The soaps have too many foreign accents already."

Grace chuckled, and a drop of sweat dripped off her nose. "But isn't there a way we can let the Agency deal with it?"

"Are you still hung up on that? No, those wannabes at Langley have shown they're done with us. Let me call Aleksander; I'll suggest I might be able to help with a role after all. Explain the producer and I are frat brothers. There'll be new rewrites for future episodes requiring someone with an accent. His reaction will let me know if he sent the note."

"You aren't gonna strong-arm him, are you? I'm telling you I want nothing more to do with killing. One time was enough. I still have nightmares."

"Of course not. I'll just pay him off." Nick gazed out at the ball field at Jimmie and Josh, smiled as he thought about Megan, and felt the sun's rays and the lie soak into his body.

Nick set the Ford's air conditioning at sixty-eight degrees and turned on the seat cooling feature. He was so furious, heat pulsed down to his toes. *I know that sonovabitch sent Grace the note.* When Aleksander opened the passenger door, the evening air rolled in, sending the air conditioning unit up to maximum.

The door slammed, and Aleksander exclaimed in a hoarse voice, "Well, Nick, let's talk about what happened in Sirte. The Company had me there keeping an eye on you."

"You were our backup? Who knew you were even trained!"

"Yeah, and I took pictures. Nice close-ups of you and your partner changing into militia uniforms. And an execution well after that raghead was taken prisoner. You'll be hung out to dry. But no need to share them with the Agency, especially now since the bastards terminated me."

"You too?" Nick tried to sound sympathetic.

"We're almost in the same boat, but until my career is as good as yours, you get to be my meal ticket. Look, all I want is some money to tide me over until you can get me a steady gig on your soap. Like I said on the phone, just fifty K until the paychecks roll in." He stared at Nick with pleading emerald eyes.

Nick felt his chest tighten. "Why are you coming to us? We're out of the game."

"I'm not getting the work, and my agent dumped me."

"But you can get a job. You have talent; why us?"

"Because you're an easy target."

"OK, I'll talk to the producer. He's a fraternity brother. But this time only. Helping you only works once."

"I promise this is it. I won't ask anything from you again."

You sure won't… Nick gritted his teeth as he continued, "It'll take more than a couple of days to get that much cash unobtrusively. How about if I get you twenty soon and the rest, and an audition, by next week, latest?"

"OK, but you don't get the master video recording until I get the gig. Not a guest appearance, but a series regular. Plus, I want my own trailer, and I want to see the story treatment as soon as it's ready."

"No problem. The producer and I are tight." Nick said with a false smile, "I assume you got the master locked up in a safe place?"

"Sure do. Safely stashed away at home."

What an ass. Crappy actor too. Is he that stupid?

"Want to see it again?" Aleksander held up his iPhone.

Nick dug his fingers and palms into the steering wheel, "No... I was there; I don't need to see it again. You've made your point."

∼

Nick and Grace found time to meet when the director got sick, and they were all told to go home after lunch. They needed the tryst at the extended-stay hotel to focus on the situation.

Nick panted as he regained his breath. *Well, even an afternoon delight has lost its charm.* Grace sprawled on her back, sweat covering her body. He dozed off into oblivion on the hotel's memory foam bed.

Grace's voice woke Nick from a sensual slumber. "So, the son-of-a-bitch wants a cash payoff and a part? You realize this could cost us our families, our livelihood, and our lives?" Grace said.

Nick's foggy brain tried to make sense out of why Megan was talking about a payoff. He shook and cleared his head as he realized it was Grace.

"And he's got a video?" she added. "We've got families to protect."

Nick propped himself up on the pillows.

"Yeah, you know the video that surfaced with the militia torturing Gaddafi."

"Yes, it was unforgettable."

"Well, Aleksander filmed a version the media never saw."

"Does it show us?"

"You bet. Shows you and me changing into *Misratan* militia uniforms and putting on balaclavas. Then of the execution clearly after he's been taken prisoner. Aleksander's threatening to take it to the press."

"I think we really should let the Agency deal with him."

"Nope, if we want to avoid the wolves, we've got to take care of this ourselves. The Agency will just let the criminal justice system deal with us."

Nick stretched while Grace paced around the hotel room naked.

He recognized this pattern. She was working herself up for what they had to do.

"OK, how do you think we should stop him?" Grace stopped pacing and snarled, "I don't want to go to prison for murdering that scummy raghead after he was captured."

Nick thought, *and a trial in the states. Megan will know what I did, what I was. It'd be the end.*

Grace continued her rant. "We'll be on the evening news for weeks… we'll end up in a federal pen."

"Couldn't we wave at each other in the exercise yard?"

Glaring at him, Grace continued to stalk around the room. "Christ, it's hot in here." She scanned the walls for a thermostat, marched over, and made an adjustment. The air conditioning created a cold wind.

Grace persisted in her indoor hike until she landed in front of the kitchen refrigerator. She opened the door, "Nothing cool to drink." As she slammed the door, she turned to him and said, "Nick, we need to take action." The cold and excitement had caused a tantalizing reaction in her nipples.

He recognized Grace's blood lust building to tackle a mission.

Grace ran over to the bed, straddled Nick, inserting him, and began a rhythmic motion. "Nick, we can't let that pecker-head get away with this."

She continued the rant through her undulations. "We've got to know we got all the copies of the recording."

Grace increased the ferocity of her movements until the mattress moved.

"Nick, we'll never be able to live without looking over our shoulders as long as that son-of-a-bitch walks the earth. I can't operate that way!"

Groping and grasping, Grace groaned, "OK, OK, I want that son-of-a-bitch dead. You hear me, D – E – A – D, dead."

Grace cried out with increasing excitement as she rode Nick like a rodeo bronco, "We're gonna do this, we're gonna do this, we're gonna do this together," and she thrust herself down.

She rose, pumped up and down in a frantic self-indulgent

demonstration of lust. She grabbed Nick's head between her hands, pulled his hair down toward his shoulders, and screamed, "You still love me enough to kill him?"

With the question hanging in the air, Grace shrieked, digging her nails into Nick's neck and tightening her knees around his torso. She yelled again, and what Nick heard was, "Do you love Megan enough to kill him?"

Nick roared "Yes," grimacing as he released and arched his back, thrusting himself deeper.

Grace sighed a long, deliciously shuddering sigh and sank softly down into Nick's embrace. For a moment, she rested her head on Nick's chest; her eyes closed in feline contentment.

With a start, Grace sat straight up and shouted, "We're gonna make that son-of-a-bitch wish he never fucked with us." She jumped off Nick and raced to the bathroom saying, "He's gonna regret screwing with us, make no mistake."

Nick lay, limp-dicked, on his pillow. *Dammit, I have to go back to my old self — the Twins ride again.*

~

Reclining in his chair some days later at CBS Television City, Studio 33, Nick read the Hollywood Reporter's front page.

Actor Dead at Scene of Fire

Assassin's Vendetta actor Aleksander Noli, who was 29 years old, was found dead on the rain-soaked driveway outside his blazing home by the Valley Bureau first responders.

Noli was pronounced dead at the scene, although the Los Angeles County Coroner has yet to determine the cause of death.

Noli's home burned to the ground due to a lightning strike from the evening's storm, although investigators from the LA County Fire Department are still on the scene. Due to the delay in getting fire vehicles through the locked security gate, the buildings were a complete loss.

A statement from his spokeswoman released on Sunday said: "Actor Aleksander Noli was killed in a freak accident early this morning. His family requests you respect their privacy at this time."

Grace came over and sat in the adjoining chair. "So, I think we're free after today's shoot."

"Yep, I want to watch Josh's school play." He paused, then said, "I think we're all finished."

> Slightly different versions have been published in: *Rizal Journal*, Issue 1 (December 28, 2016): 10-21; *The Criterion eJournal*, Vol. 7, Issue VI (December 2016), 377-384; *Anthology Askew Volume 003: Askew Adventures*, Mandy Melanson, Dusty Grein, & Emma T. Gitani, eds., North Charleston, SC: CreateSpace, July 2, 2017, pp. 25-34; and in *Love, Sweet to Spicy: A Corrales Writing Group Anthology*, Patricia Walkow, ed., North Charleston, SC: CreateSpace, January 2018, pp. 3-11. Awarded Third Place in the New Mexico Press Women, New Mexico Communication 2018 Contest, Essay, Chapter, or Section in a Book.

A TRIANGLE WITH TWO SIDES

MAHENDRA WAGHELA

My job happens to be more boring than the most, but that day was something entirely out of my playbook.

I woke up too early and got ready in a tearing hurry. Somehow, I drove around the main roads to avoid the mad morning traffic and reached the opposite outskirts of the bursting Bangalore city. I reached the spot earlier than most of my tribe would. Today, I needed to finish the work fast and reach home in time. My wife would be impossible to deal with if I missed her mawkish anniversary party routine. The special ordeal included suffering her smelly south-Indian friends and unbelievably loud, infantile cousins ready with their vapid jokes spared for the special occasion. These were the people more enthused about our anniversary than their own.

No one in that billing route had come forward to warn me about this place and, of course, I didn't bother to ask. With a sour taste in my mouth, I parked my bike in the distance because it kept on skidding on the dry gravel and walked the rest of the dirt track. The time was 9am or so when I entered the old, crumbling building to check the meter readings and bill the owners. As these kinds of buildings go, billing meters are placed under the staircase to protect the privacy of owners. Or they were fitted in the dingy corner of parking basements for easy access for repairmen and for billing people like me, who have to take the current reading of usage, prepare the bills and drop them in their respective letter boxes.

Who would construct an apartment building in this abandoned, semi-wilderness was beyond my senses, but then, the real estate boom of the millennium that never reached this side of the city was never considered a rational phenomenon. I stepped forward. The front garden was dried, the lawn all around me was yellowed beyond repair and the fountain pool had no water. All brass taps were stolen, baring one. The front desk was rusted and mangled beyond recognition. There was no sign of life in the security cabin to check or guide me to the meters. I climbed down the broken steps into the deserted basement. Most cars were covered under layers of fine dust. A few of them stood there as if forgotten for years. A neglected scooter had so much dust on top of it that it was impossible to make out its original color, and the tires were almost melted and pulverized by the salt in the air.

Ah! That was the exact moment when I realized that the place was unusually silent for a resident building at this time of morning. I could hear the faint traffic noises from the main road that was at least five kilometers from the dirt track I traveled to reach here.

No matter, I took a deep breath and reached the cobwebbed cabinet enclosure to look for the electric utility meters. The glass cases were broken. Only one meter for apartment No 770 was intact. It was running at a frantic speed, as if someone's heater, geysers, refrigerators, ACs, irons, ceiling fans, generators and whatnot were going on all out, full blast. I heard a sharp horn from the road and an old-model lime green Fiat in gleaming condition pulled in with a flourish. It stopped under the parking spot marked 770.

I pulled out my bill book to enter the details: customer name, utility number, billing cycle, time and Date, my employee log book number, building number and meter number, and area. Apartment 770's meter was still whirring at such a speed that I couldn't make out the last three digits, let alone the whole eight digit number. I had

A TRIANGLE WITH TWO SIDES

the previous bill's digits that had to be subtracted from the current one to arrive at the month's billing amount. I don't know how much time passed looking at the spinning digits but the vrooming car engine shook my insides out. The bill book fell from my hands but I somehow managed to gain my balance.

The lime green Fiat's door opened and a young woman in tight jeans and halter neck white top walked out. I felt grateful for the presence of another human being and turned to check the meter again. Of course it was impossible to take down the current reading.

"Are you from the Citylimits Power Utility?" The woman's voice was brisk, almost rude.

"Yes. No one else residing in this building? All the meters are stopped or broken!"

"You haven't been here before? Mine is 770." She pointed her key at the steps and waved her loaded grocery bag in a smooth dancing move.

"No, my first time here."

"That meter is not working. I have a new one fitted in my apartment. Come, let's climb the steps, the elevator hasn't been working here for some time."

I swallowed my grunt and followed her. I am 38 and have a sweet wife and a seven year old prankster for a daughter, but I stared in the way any man would. Even without those killer stilettos, the woman was at least an inch taller than me, and her walk had the grace and confidence of a seasoned ramp model. Her jeans were so tight that the micro size panties were clearly outlined under the indigo fabric. She had her lustrous black hair tinted and coiffed to perfection, reaching just short of her flaring hips. No bra under her thin top. On the second step, her top slipped upwards, revealing her buttery smooth skin and a light brown mole the size of a pearl gleamed on her left hip. I almost missed a step, tumbled and held on the railing as she shouted, "Careful there!"

She thrust her car keys into her hip pocket and pulled out a bunch of jingling keys. Her strawberry red fingernails shone in the daylight streaming through the shaft in the wall. I almost fell forward to grab her gorgeous ass. Had she turned her head at the moment, I had my bill book hiding my unbelievable erection. Ironically, last night my wife had tried hard and I remained as limp as an overripe banana. I pumped up to catch up with the speed of the hot bomb climbing ahead of me.

With each step, our distance narrowed, and I am not talking about the distance between our bodies. Maybe it was an overtly familiar, magical scent about her that drew me in. There was something like known warmth and strange vibrations, as if I knew her for years. The weirdest thing was that I had no idea what her face was like, but I felt assured: it was agreeable, attractive, stunning, irresistible.

Years back, I had a crazy argument about this aspect of animal magnetism with my wife. A few weeks after our marriage, my wife had caught me ogling a young collegian girl while waiting at a bus-stop and she had asked me in her point blank, blunt manner, "What if the girl that walked past us had a hideous face? Pimpled, maybe blistered or even burnt and cruelly disfigured?" She yanked me away and we hailed a taxi that evening. Of course, I never got to see that girl's face. But at night my wife announced a bedroom curfew when I insisted that, I was sure, the girl's face would be stunningly attractive.

"No logic in your long-winded, spineless amoeba arguments," my wife shot back and we ended up on the opposite sides of our ornate double bed.

Back to now. Back to the job of following the shapely woman in the old building to finish my billing work. We reached the landing to her apartment 770. She unlocked the front door and, without bothering to look at me, waved me in. She flung her keys on a peg on the wall and said, "The meter is in the front bedroom, you see the yellow door there?"

That bedroom was a strange place to fit an utility electric meter, more so if it was fitted after the external one in the basement was knocked out. It was also against the government regulation.

"No one else is staying in this building?" I asked and looked around. The apartment was straight out of my daydream; it was huge, squeaky clean and flooded with the afternoon sunlight falling from the spacious balcony. White gossamer curtains were pulled sideways. The TV unit took up half the wall and looked like a home theatre with three sets of oversized speakers. A giant white conch sat on the center table. Above my head, a crystal chandelier reflected the daylight like a cluster of giant diamonds.

"Meter is on the left side of the bed," she shouted and bent over to reach into her grocery bag. Her white top slipped up again, her jeans slid down along her wide tapering hips to reveal her pale pink lace panties. I stopped in my stride and, after a moment of hesitation, went to the yellow bedroom door.

"This one?" I stood beside the door that was half way open.

"Push it, push it open," she shouted without turning. I fumbled with my bill book and pen. My hands were shaking as I vaguely realized that I had not seen the face of the woman who was telling me to enter one of her bedrooms! Feeling the itchy warmth of sweat in my armpits, I pushed the door in.

In a complete contrast to the lavish drawing room, this was an unusually cramped and dark room. The plaster on the walls had peeled off and hideous stains ran along the walls. Cheap window curtains were drawn to the floor. I took a moment to realize that someone was asleep, face down, covered under a blanket on a rusted iron double bed, not unlike mine at home. I felt uneasy. I didn't even look for the meter and tuned to run out but the door slammed shut in place. I twisted the brass handle, but there was no point. A resounding click convinced me that I was locked inside.

"Are you there? Is that you who fixed me in? Hey...?" I screamed in panic, my words sounded barely coherent to me, let alone to someone beyond the locked door.

I banged on the door, but there was no answer. Dark circles floated in front of me as I felt myself leaning against the wall and in a dreamy slow motion state until my head banged hard on the floor. A few minutes must have passed in between, but finally I felt the icy cold tiles through my shirt. My eyes remained closed in a strange calm as I waited for the maddening palpitations in my chest to subside. I was still shaking inside and my hands felt numb, as if after holding heavy dumbbells for too long. With a conscious effort, I opened my eyes, like waking up from a deep slumber, and dared to look around. My bill book was upside down, lying next to one leg of the bed. The angular cap of the pen I saw for sure. I felt too tired to look for the pen.

After an excruciating moment of dizziness, I could make out some things in the dim outline, but I was locked in that same spot because my left leg was folded under my right leg. The blood in my veins turned to ice as the blanketed figure lying on the bed shifted and a smooth feminine leg sled out. I closed my eyes and opened again to make sure of what I was seeing. The leg slid out, up to the knee, and turned. What I noticed was the silver ring on the second toe. It was a right leg and the ring was a slim dead ringer snake; the familiar shape registered gently as if I was heavily sedated. I decided to sit in the quiet of the place until my head stopped spinning like a crazy cartwheel. I looked on, mesmerized by the exposed feminine leg with a silver snake ring on the second toe. I hit upon some kind of clarity and courage in that strange moment.

"Dolly," I blurted in a voice that sounded strangled and weak. "Dolly…" I tried to scream in that same unfamiliar voice.

Finally I managed to get up from the floor and settled on the plush bed. I pulled the blanket gently upward and noticed the telltale pearl size brown mole on her left hip. I touched the mole to see if it was a mere stain to fool me in the semidarkness. It was real. It didn't disappear as I rubbed it a little. I kissed the mole with all-consuming passion.

"Dolly, is this your weird, magnified love? Your stupid way to make me a fool in a nightmare like this?" I croaked.

"May I please?" With infinite slowness and care, I pushed open her silk top, millimeter by millimeter until I reached her taught bra strap. "Hey," I mumbled and gently unhooked her satin bra. I reached from both sides and lovingly held her throbbing milk balloons. She let out an involuntary moan, probably a half-hearted approval. Her skin trembled against mine, but I still didn't feel sure. I kissed her back and finally her neck. "Time to turn over sweetheart, I am hard and burning," I said in the softest voice possible. "Show me your face, please…"

I reached under her musky naval and massaged her warm pubic mound. That always did the trick. So far. I pulled at her panties as she raised herself a little and let out a deep, strangled sigh.

"Please dear," I massaged her firm inner thighs with my other hand to wake up her sure-fire erroneous zone. "Show your face and assure me, please?" I repeated and felt her moist vulva. "Please, my Dolly dessert…"

"Did you see her face?" My wife asked, not yet bothering to remove the pillow from her face.

"Whose face?"

"Don't you play innocent Jack with me! Remember the list of your fetishes? Lime green retro Fiat, for heaven's sake! Black stilettos, what can be triter? Ridiculously tight jeans on a grown woman, did you ever grow up after school? Pink lace panties, done to death in tacky romcoms, yuck, yuck, YUCK! Semi-transparent white top without bra, really? Common boy, I'm talking about the composite bundle of tired cliché, the one who locked you in!"

"No, of course not. I haven't seen her face, I swear!"

"I swear, my ass! You didn't see her face, or she refused to show it to you?"

There was only one way out of this complicated mess. "What do you want me to do, Dolly dear? Fall on the floor on my knees and beg for mercy?" I leaned over one side, ready to hit the light switch on the wall.

She removed the pillow from her face. Her eyes shone with evil glee as she spoke in her huskiest, tightest whisper. "Gimme that lip lock without switching on the overhead lights, you know it kills my mood and my need for the dark side of romance." Dolly slapped my hand away from the light switch.

I had heard that familiar demand before in that same, sickeningly familiar voice. I obeyed like a henpecked husband.

LOVERS IN HIDING

SUZANNE BAGINSKIE

"Sally, don't wish for a husband, your chances of getting married are slim and none," Dad said, before I blew out the candles at my thirty-ninth birthday party. All my family and friends broke into laughter. Rage filled me. I forced a smile as they whispered among themselves. Had I become the family joke? Dad had warned me and more than once – I'd probably turn out to be an old maid. Last time I counted, I only had two boyfriends since high school and neither of those relationships blossomed. But now, I can't help thinking remaining single might not be so bad, especially after the dire situation I found myself in that fateful Friday night.

Monday evening at the thrift shop where I worked, a customer raced in through the doorway around closing time. I forced a smile. He frantically searched the action/adventure DVD's shelf and finally chose one. He approached, set the movie on the countertop between us and I couldn't help but notice his striking aqua-blue eyes. He handed me a credit card. I quickly scanned it and his name, Jake Miles appeared on my computer screen.

"This is a great action video, Mr. Miles," I said, pushing my brunette bangs across my forehead. He smiled and gazed at my name badge.

"Sally. I'm Jake. I've heard good reviews about this film from my students."

Hearing my name pronounced by his husky voice awakened a hidden surge of adrenaline that shot through me like a wildfire in a dry forest. Beside those sexy eyes, he had ash-blond hair and an athletic build. It must have been a mutual attraction because he lingered and chatted on.

He'd attended Woodview High School too, graduating three years ahead of me. We discussed our memories of the teachers we both liked and disliked. His interests included football games, movies, and pizza. Same as mine. We certainly had a lot in common. I was impressed when he mentioned he taught chemistry at the local college in town.

So well educated and handsome, his wonderful eyes sparkled at me. My cheeks warmed. I felt giddy as a schoolgirl inside and yearned for more. I couldn't understand why I was instantly attracted to him – I usually remained immune to men. His eyes glazed over me and more than once, sending a ripple of excitement tingling beneath my skin. Not wanting it to end, I finally said, "It's closing time, so I'll have to ask you to leave now."

"Would it be all right if I walk you home?" he asked eagerly.

My mind thought of all the good reasons why he shouldn't. I recalled the rigid principals I'd established to avoid being hurt again. One by one, they were slipping away as those magnificent eyes focused directly into mine. "Okay," I gushed. "It'll take about five minutes to shut this place down and I'll need you to wait outside."

"No problem," he answered.

When he reached for his purchase, I secretly checked his left hand for a wedding band. His ring finger was naked and had no missing tan line. After he sauntered through the doorway, pulling it tightly shut behind him, I walked over and secured the lock. I headed to the rear of the store with the day's receipts. Pausing for a moment, I had second thoughts. I turned and peered out at him from the back office. Jake's tall muscular form leaned against the glass panes. I could hardly believe he was waiting for me. His champagne-colored hair glistened beneath the fluorescent store's sign that hung brightly above him. The more I studied the guy, the more my heart flip-flopped in response. His interest in me seemed genuine and I trusted my instincts. I spun the safe's dial and, when I reached the front door, switched off the lights. Once outside, I locked the top bolt and double-checked the knob.

Reeling around, I flashed a smile at Jake. "I live in the Baywood Apartments on Meadows Avenue; it's about four blocks north of here."

"I know the area, I checked them out a few years ago when I was apartment hunting. Ready?" I nodded.

We walked along in the cool October breeze on dimly lit streets, Jake clutching the bag with his left hand.

"How long have you been working in the thrift store?" he asked.

"Five years. I started as a clerk and now I manage the store for the owner. He's retired."

"I bet you see a lot of antiques and junk come through."

"There are so many stories I could tell you. One great advantage is having first pick of the donated books and movies."

"I like reading, but mostly mysteries and thrillers." He smiled a lot. We conversed easily.

Arriving at the apartment building's front door, I said, "Jake, would you like to come in and warm up with some hot coffee?" I couldn't believe I'd become so bold.

"That sounds great."

We climbed the stairs to the second level. I unlocked the door and he followed me into the kitchen. "Have a seat. It won't take long to brew."

"Need any help?" he asked, before sitting on a chair.

"No thanks." I placed the filter and grounds inside the coffee pot and remembered the fresh apple pie in the refrigerator. I mentally patted myself on the back for having baked it earlier. Soon the aroma of fresh coffee perked in the air. All the while, I knew his eyes were on me.

"Coffee's ready. Would you like a piece of homemade apple pie?"

"Wow, that sounds great."

A sexy grin rose on his lips, making my body temperature rise. I dished out two pieces and poured steaming coffee into our cups. Together, we carried our mugs to the den and sat on my worn blue velvet sofa in front of the TV. I'd wished I had the money to replace it, but he didn't seem to notice my meager surroundings.

"This pie is delicious, almost as good as my mother's."

"Thanks, I'll take that as a compliment. Shall I put your film in?"

"Yes."

The coffee warmed us, and the small talk continued. He seemed more interested in me than the movie. A half hour later, Jake leaned over and planted a simple kiss on my lips. He pressed lightly at first and then became more demanding. His arms encircled my back, pulling me closer, and I eagerly slid my arms around him as if swept away by a tide of mounting emotions. The mahogany end tables held our forgotten mugs. Instead, we drank in the intoxication of each other's kisses. The DVD played on to an unobserving audience. He kissed my neck, and nibbled on my ear, before his lips and tongue slid into my mouth again.

I'd never thought I'd let another man get this close to me, after two failed affairs and the awful hurt that followed. Jake's lips awakened a deeply, hidden need I had tried to permanently bury.

The movie ended and the TV blanked. We both flinched.

Jake glanced at his watch. "I better be going, it's getting late."

"It is." I rose to eject the DVD from my player and then handed it to him. We inched toward the doorway, holding hands. Neither of us wanted to say good-bye. He pushed open the door, and I walked to the building entrance with him. Once outside, the moonlight illuminated our last kiss.

He hugged me and whispered, "Can I see you tomorrow night?" I caught an inkling of his concern for me, and I knew I wanted to know more about him, too.

"Yes. I'm working nine to five the rest of this week." My heart hammered inside, was this really happening?

Every day, Jake came in at quitting time and walked me home. I'd prepare special dinners for the two of us, and afterwards, we'd snuggle in the den. Jake praised my cooking abilities and compared me to his mom, whose cooking he loved. At times, I wondered why he never took me out to eat, but Jake's excuse was he hated restaurants. I had to stretch my food budget, but Jake pitched in, purchasing bottles of wine and special desserts. Each night we put on a popular TV show but ended up making out instead.

I'd convinced myself, he never took me anywhere because he wanted me all to himself. In my heart, I had some doubts. Nonetheless, I hiked to work each day in awe. I never believed I'd find someone like Jake and the relationship grew stronger each day. Now and then I'd reflect on my dad's words. I'd show him and my family they were wrong once I knew Jake's real intentions. I was falling in love with him, but I needed more time. I had those same feelings for the last guy who trampled my heart. I hoped this third chance at love would be a charm.

Three weeks later, Jake carried me into my bedroom. Gently, he laid me on the bed. We kissed and hugged each other tightly for a few moments.

"Are you okay with this?" he asked.

"Yes," I whispered breathlessly.

Taking his time, he undressed me. Piece by piece, the tips of his fingers lingered in all the right places. Shivers of delight swept through me. Once I was completely naked, Jake stood. He tore off his shirt and pants, settling back on the mattress next to me.

"You're beautiful," he murmured in a husky voice. He kissed a path of kisses on my lips, neck, and down to my breasts, cuddling them. Every caress spread the heat through my body and each touch carried the flame of desire. I inhaled his spicy scent and ran my fingers along his well-developed muscular chest, the sensation of his growing hardness pressing against my stomach.

His mouth lingered on my nipples. They puckered in response. We continued to explore each other's bodies until neither of us could hold back. He cradled my hips and slipped inside me, gyrating in a slow rhythm at first. When he tilted my bottom slightly, a soft groan escaped his lips, and we moved even faster until the tremors subsided. He collapsed alongside me. Breathing heavy, our physical needs were now satisfied as our passion slowly released itself.

My former sexual experiences had been in the back seat of a car. My boyfriend kissed me a couple of times and then forced himself on me. The sessions left me feeling dirty and used. Jake kindled a craving inside me, one I'd never known existed. The best part came later that night when he whispered those three little words into my ear. "I love you."

Could I believe what I'd just heard? I repeated them back and meant it with all my heart and soul. We kissed. I had hope, maybe I could bring him to the next family gathering, wouldn't my dad be surprised.

Everything was going great, or so I thought, until Wednesday night. Jake waited for me to close up the shop, prompt as usual around nine. The weather was colder, and he drove me home in his Chevy van. I noticed his face had a chalky cast and his brows knit together hard, creating wrinkles on his forehead. He barely spoke. We held hands and trudged toward my apartment in silence. Maybe he had a bad day teaching. I figured he'd mention it at dinner. He didn't.

He continued acting withdrawn and quiet as I cleaned the dishes. I sent him into the den. I was worried. Had he met someone else and didn't know how to tell me? Self-doubt clouded my mind and I brushed away tears before I joined him on the couch. I went to kiss him, but he pushed me away and his words tumbled out.

"Sally, I have something to confess."

I braced myself for the worst, my shoulders slumped against the sofa.

"I'm married. My wife's name is Diane. But I've fallen in love with you."

My chest heaved with a loud sob. Tears trickled down my cheeks. Confused, my mind refused to register the significance of his words. I turned away and covered my ears. I didn't want to listen, but he continued on.

"Diane is not at all like you. She's heartless and cold. You're warm, loving, and everything I need. But, she's my wife. She'd sworn to never divorce me. It's complicated. When her father passes away, he leaves her a healthy trust fund with one stipulation, she has to be married in order to receive the inheritance. We made reciprocal wills stating that if either one survives the other, the trust fund becomes theirs. My only asset is my teacher's 401 K pension plan and, if we divorce, Diane, by law, is entitled to half. I don't mean to hurt you, but at this point in our relationship, I felt you needed to know the truth. I can never marry you."

His last statement stung me as if someone slapped my face hard. My lower lip trembled, my stomach churned. I leaped from the sofa, "Jake, please leave, I have to think," I sobbed loudly as I tried to deal with the familiar heartache. I guess he understood. I closed my eyes for a few seconds and soon heard the front door shut.

I cried out, "Why me... why do I deserve to be hurt time after time?" I kept repeating those words. "I can never marry you." Thoughts of loneliness filled me, and my heart thumped uncontrollably. Oh Jake, how could this have happened. Why did you lead me on? I yielded to the compulsive tears that racked my body. Eventually I fell asleep curled up on the sofa.

The next morning when I awoke. I pressed ice cubes in a folded dish towel against my swollen eyes. The thought of food turned my stomach. I comforted myself with hot tea. Every time I thought of Jake, I'd wept.

Scheduled for the night shift, I swallowed hard, showered, and dressed. On the walk there, I hoped work would make me forget the painful memory of last night. I kept myself busy logging in the latest donations, sorting, and shelving them. Deep inside, I knew I still loved him, even after his confession. It all made sense to me now, why he never took me anywhere. He didn't want to take the chance his wife might find out.

Jake stayed away for two solid weeks. It gave me time to come to terms with the situation. Saturday evening right before closing, he caught me off guard. A customer stood at the counter when Jake strolled in wearing a sheepish grin.

"Hello, I'll be right with you," I said, my heart pounding hard against my ribs at the sight of him.

"Take your time," he answered, and the hearty tone of his voice teased me. I bagged the man's purchase and handed him change. He turned and exited the store.

Jake and I were totally alone. I swallowed hard and forced myself to stay strong. He strolled to the counter and his smile was irresistible.

"Sally, I've missed you so much I'd like to see you again. Can you forgive me?" When he spoke, his voice was tender, almost like a small child pleading. My thoughts filtered back to the day I'd first met him, while my body betrayed me aching for his touch. How could I refuse?

"Jake, I've missed you too," I blurted.

"Can I drive you home tonight? We need to talk."

I hesitated, but my heart wouldn't let me say no. "Okay, I'll need to close up first. Please wait outside."

I followed my normal routine, locked the shop's door behind me and entered his car. When we arrived at my apartment, he held my hand on the way in. My heart pounded and desire filled me.

"Sally, I'm sorry I didn't tell you I was married that first night, everything happened so fast."

"You weren't wearing a wedding ring, so I naturally assumed you weren't."

"I know, I removed it a couple of years ago. Diane and I maintain the same house, but our marriage is a farce. Can you accept me on those terms? You're the one I love."

I had been so miserable since that night he confessed and had decided marriage must not be in the cards for me. So, I grabbed at the only thing that could replace the gloom and loneliness of the last two weeks – Jake. "Yes," I whispered. All the feelings I had denied flooded back into my heart.

He led me straight to my bedroom and undressed me. We kissed and our tongues collided once again. His hands roamed every inch of my body, and his lips played with my nipples and roamed lower. I tugged at his clothing and soon felt the heat of his passion. Once he thrust inside me, any thoughts of his wife were erased. We slipped into our affair again, like nothing ever happened. We were lovers in hiding.

Two weeks passed. Our arms were wrapped around each other after sex, and I said, "I love you Jake, so very much. I'd do anything for you." I fondled his cheek and stared into his aqua-blue eyes.

Jake stared back and answered, "Anything?" His smile became an evil grin before he repeated, "I love you too."

The next evening, we watched a movie together. It had a simple murder scheme, the husband poisoned his wife. Jake turned to me when it ended and said, "That could be the perfect solution to our problem, Sally. If we dispose of my wife, we can be together forever."

Shocked. I wondered if I heard him correctly. "What? I don't want to go to jail, Jake," I answered. Yes, I was jealous of Diane, but there was no way I'd think about murdering her. Jake carried on our conversation even further.

"The annual teachers convention will be held at the local hotel next week. You could apply to work at their seminar training section. With all your clerking experience, I'm sure they'd hire you."

"I certainly could use the extra money," I answered, wondering what he was hinting at.

"After the lights are dimmed, and the film is rolling, you could add poison to my wife's drink cup. She loves diet cola. During intermission, we'd come over and each order one." His face remained calm.

Was I understanding him correctly? I inhaled and my emotions flickered between the sense of right and wrong and my love for Jake. He reached over and kissed me passionately, sending waves of burning sensations vibrating through my body. I opened my eyes and found myself becoming tempted, it all sounded so easy.

"What kind of poison?" I cringed at the word.

Jake smiled and hugged me. "Don't worry about it, I majored in chemistry. All you have to do is stir it into her drink before you serve her. When the poison takes effect, I'll play the devoted husband and take care of the rest." He made it sound so easy. I felt myself being convinced. Jake made love to me that night and while he tempted me with physical desire, my defenses weakened. I allowed him to tear away a piece of my moral soul. I agreed. He promised we'd be together forever, and at that moment I was too powerless to resist.

The next day I drove to the college office and filled out an application. The lady glanced over my experience and took me into another office for an interview. The job was for Friday night. I knew I could switch my schedule with Delores, the dayshift person – she owed me a favor.

I'd answered all their questions correctly, and two days later my phone rang.

"Sally Jenkins," a strange woman's voice asked.

"Yes."

"I'm Mrs. Morgan, I interviewed you on Monday at the convention center."

"Of course." I tightened my grip on the receiver.

"You've been selected for the position if you still want it. You'll start at six o'clock on Friday evening."

"Thank you, I'll be there." Excited, I hung up the phone. I couldn't wait to relay the news to Jake. But before long, a cold chill of alarm spread through me and reminded me of his plan.

When Jake arrived that evening, I blurted out, "I got the job, they called today."

"That's wonderful," Jake whispered. A strange, eager look flashed in his eyes. His arms swept me close, and he gently kissed my lips.

"Jake, I'm not sure I can do it," I stammered.

He ignored me and said, "I love you so much. This way we can wait a few months and then get married." He buried his face in my hair and nuzzled my neck, making my pulse throb. He carried me to the bedroom, and I became hypnotized by his touch. The sweet intoxicating musk of his body overwhelmed me. Our bodies were in exquisite harmony, and we soared together into a hot wave of passion. I had never felt more loved and secure.

Afterwards, we lay entwined with each other. I talked about planning a small wedding for all my friends and family to attend. He sounded pleased. They would all be in awe as I'd finally reveal my precious Jake to them. I knew they would love him as much as I did, and the laugh would be on them this time. I smoothed my hair, my fingers shaking. Somehow, I'd summon up the courage to do his bidding, so the two of us could be together forever.

On Thursday, the night before the convention, we decided to confirm the details. Jake told me the poison would be inside a small capsule and have no odor or taste. I'd open it discreetly and stir it in while everyone was viewing the training movie. Diane would never notice anything different about her cola, and the poison would travel quickly through her blood stream. Jake said it was impossible to trace, even if an autopsy were performed. I fretted, but he reassured me of his love. His lips and hands were more persuasive than I cared to admit. He said it wouldn't be long before we would never have to say good-bye.

The night of the convention finally came, and my pulse raced. Following the plan, I arrived at the hotel early and entered the screening room. My first duty was to set up the equipment. I hid the fateful capsule inside my blouse pocket. My hands started to shake as I stuck the film into the DVD machine. I pressed the button and lowered the movie screen.

Soon, attendees wandered in and chose a seat. I glanced at Jake and his wife when they entered the room. I faked any sign of recognition. The hotel waiters finished setting up the beverages and snacks and exited. A speaker announced the first session of the training film – my cue. I hit the play button. As the room darkened, I waited behind the snack table, opened the capsule, trickled the poison into an empty cup and set it aside.

Thirty minutes later, the lights signaled intermission. I paused the DVD player and went to stand behind the refreshment table. One by one, attendees came over, and I served them their choice of beverage. When Jake and his wife asked for drinks, I acted as natural as possible and reached for that lethal cup. A dull ache of foreboding surfaced; I breathed deeply and then slowly exhaled. The room buzzed with chatter until the lights dimmed for the second half. Everyone settled into their seats again. I restarted the film. A small bead of sweat formed on my forehead. I dabbed at it with a napkin.

After thirty minutes the screen went blank again and the lights switched on. People commented on the details of the session. Jake rose unsteadily from his chair. He staggered toward the snack table but collapsed on the conference room floor. I meagerly approached as the crowd rushed to gather around him. Someone hollered, "Dial 911."

His wife Diane crept up beside me, and together we peered at him lying helpless on the floor. He moved his lips to speak, but the words wouldn't form. I noticed the realization in his aqua-blue eyes before he passed out with the two of us staring down at him.

Only the day before, I happened to drive by the college in the thrift shop's truck. I noticed Jake's van leaving the parking lot. I followed him in heavy traffic, hoping to catch up and say hello. He drove to a local shopping mall, and parked next to a blue Toyota with an attractive redhead seated inside. The strange woman dashed from her car and raced straight to his van. Once inside, she smothered his lips with an intimate kiss.

I froze. Numbed by the shock of what I'd witnessed, I watched Jake restart his van and drive to the other side of town. I trailed behind them at a leisurely, unnoticeable speed, tears soaking my cheeks. They parked and disappeared inside a cheap motel. I'd seen enough and sped home.

There was only one thing I could do. I contacted Jake's wife, Diane. She met me at a local diner, and we had an extensive conversation. She was nothing like the picture Jake painted of her. In fact, I expected her to hate me, but she gave me a chance to tell her my side of the story. Jake had lied to me. Together we went to the police and set the trap.

Jake was right. The poison was untraceable. The police lab said using it would surely have killed Diane. The detective supplied me with a substitute capsule, which only paralyzed Jake. But that tortured look on his face revealed he'd believed I gave him the dose of his own poison. By the time the drug wore off Diane and I had become the best of friends.

Within six months, they sentenced Jake to ten years in the county jail for attempted murder. Diane stayed married to him in name only. A year later her dad died, and she inherited her father's estate. She sought legal advice and divorced Jake, getting half of his 401K money.

She accepted the fact that Jake and I had cheated on her but credited me with saving her life. Diane had a generous nature and shared some of her wealth with me. Her funds enabled me to purchase the thrift store and establish a healthy bank account. If I hadn't discovered the redhead, things may have turned out differently. I realize now, Jake used his evil ways to control me, but in my own heart, I knew I would have never poisoned Diane.

I'm still single, my own boss and working the night shift by choice. It will take some time to get over my hurt feelings from Jake, but I found a new friend in Diane. As for my dad and family, they envy my successful business venture and respect me for succeeding all on my own.

ROMANCE ON THE IRONHORSE

O'LABUMI BROWNE

We got to CBGB's around nine that evening; a notoriously dingy hole of a club. Every inch of the stonework walls were covered with photographs of popular bands like Blondie, the Ramones, and the B-52's, pasted cheek-to-chin with hundreds of lesser-knowns and unknowns, and all of it scribbled over with decades of graffiti messages like, *hanky loves panky*, *run like hell*, *agents of the sun* and the *bar-bitch-u-ate*. The stench of cigarettes and stale beer flooding my nostrils, we made our way to a rickety wooden table and sat down.

Just as Jesse jumped up to get us some drinks, I heard the thrum of an acoustic guitar and turned towards the stage. A young, Asian-looking, black woman in tight stone-washed jeans stood under the hazy lights, sensually gyrating her hips and thighs and strumming away. Her arms were bare and finely sculpted. Her biceps were swelling and receding with the cadence of the music – a blend of blues, classical rock, and soulful funk with which she was so skillfully jazzing the air. A jewel gleamed in her navel. Her nipples, like pebbles, strained against the fabric of her T-shirt.

I felt the table wobble when Jess returned with our drinks. I reached for my mine without looking, my eyes glued to the stage.

"Man-oh-man, Cherokee (his high school nickname)," I blurted, "she's good."

"Who," Jessie giggled, "ya mean Quinn?"

My eyes went wide. "Oh my God, Cherokee," I croaked, "ya know her!?"

"Yeah," he said, with another chuckle. "I'll introduce ya after her set."

Her set lasted for five songs, and my eyes and ears hungrily devoured every second of it. Especially when she finished thanking the audience, and then pulled her tulip-red guitar strap over her magnificent swash of hair. A Mohawk-cut. Just like I had. Only hers was blessed with glorious, radiant curls that shimmered under the glow of stage lights. My knees betrayed me as I rose to my feet. I had to grab the table to steady myself before setting off for the bar at the back of the room. Before anything else, I needed another drink. It was all too much. That face! That body! That voice! That hair!

And just to think this lowly human being was about to meet her, was unimaginable.

I took the drink from the bartender and made sure I got a good pull on it before heading back to where Cherokee and I were sitting. Just as I was settling back in at our table, there was Quinn, making her way over to where we were. Our eyes locked as she neared and glided into the seat next to mine. So close, I could make out the beads of perspiration glistening in the curls of her Mohawk, and smell the China Musk she was wearing. Her upper lip was arched in an ambiguous one-sided half grin.

My heart pounded.

"Quinn, meet Dee," Cherokee blurted. "Dee, Quinn."

We shook hands.

I hardly recognized my own voice when I squeaked, "I really enjoyed listening to your music."

"Thanks," she said with a sweet smile now on her lips. "If you stick around for my next set, there's a song I'd like to play, especially for you."

Goosebumps sprouted on my arms.

I gave in to a sudden urge to look down at my shoes.

"Thank you," I sputtered.

"Damn Girl," Cherokee broke in, "your sound gets better every time I hear you!"

"I hope so," she giggled. "I'm at the studio so often I barely remember what my place looks like."

"Rumor has it that folks from Capital Records have been checking you out," Cherokee announced.

"And until I get that record deal," Quinn chuckled, glancing in my direction, "that's all they are, friend; rumors."

I punctuated my timid silence with belts of my drink as the two old friends carried on like this for several more minutes: Cherokee pelting Quinn with flattery and Quinn fending it off with good-natured modesty. Yet, more often than not, her responses were delivered with solicitous side glances my way. Almost as if... *But what on God's green earth*, I told myself, *could this goddess possibly see in the likes of me?* As I said before, it was just too much. Too much to dare hope, too much to try not to. *Oh, ye of little faith*, I imagined hearing my mother say, as she would whenever she heard me putting myself down. *You're leaping to conclusions.* I cautioned myself. *You need to get a grip. Step back. Get a little perspective.* I excused myself, fled the table, and headed for the bathroom.

In the lady's room I stopped at the sink and dabbed water on my face to cool my rising fever. Cupping my palms, I sipped water as images of the lady filled my mind; I couldn't do anything but drink her in. Her jet-black Mohawk curls, perfectly accentuating the almond shape of her eyes and enhancing her Afro-Asian features, gold G-clef earring swaying in her left ear, animating her amber skin with dancing refracted light.

A goddess!

. . .

Quinn, as sure as Jesus wore sandals, mesmerized me with the hope that our little tryst in CBGB's would be the beginning of something more. But the rational, more doubting, less confident part of me had already accepted that a fine, black, Asian beauty like Quinn had only hooked up with an ugly goose like me for the convenience of the moment. I certainly never expected her to call me up just two days later and carry on about how much she had enjoyed it all and tell me she wanted to see me again the very next weekend. And I sure as hell never imagined she'd call again, just minutes after hanging up, to tell me she just couldn't wait until next weekend and that she had to see me now.

She didn't have to ask twice.

It was a fine enough Sunday afternoon. We met in Prospect Park, where we casually strolled the grounds, engaging in the stop and go, sometimes awkward kind of conversation that people who have intimate feelings but know little about one another have.

Quinn didn't like talking about her early childhood. It wasn't until weeks later that she let on that she was born in Vietnam, and that her father – a black soldier who had been stationed there at the time – brought her to the US from Saigon to live with him, his American wife and their two children in Maryland. Yet, she ached and longed for her Vietnamese mother and had nightmares about their separation. She has since heard that her mother was now living somewhere in Manhattan's Chinatown and has been on a relentless search for her ever since.

I told her that I was at odds with my parents too. Being gay was not the problem at home. Getting high was. They worried for me and feared that my bad habits would have a negative influence on my younger brothers and sister. The one difference was that Quinn longed to live with her mother, I didn't. I moved out when I was nineteen.

There was no booze this time, just the two of us enjoying each other's company. As we stopped at Carvels, and took turns licking each other's cones, and later browsing a florist's stand, where Quinn bought two roses and stuck one of them in each of our Mohawks, I was still haunted by the feeling that I wasn't good enough or pretty enough for her. Yet, this utterly romantic stroll had me falling quicker than I believed I should for this chick.

But it was the ride home that really did it.

The D train was crowded. We couldn't sit together. So, Quinn took a seat directly opposite and across the aisle. As soon as we got comfortable, our eyes locked. I didn't mean to stare, but I couldn't not look at her. I was enchanted by one black curl, shaped like an upside-down question mark that drooped from her Mohawk and encircled her eyebrow, and I was delighted by the G-clef in her right ear and guitar in her left, both swaying with the cadence of the train.

She watched me.

Satisfied that she had my attention, she relaxed her back against the seat as my eyes surveyed her plaid cotton shirt, where a few buttons had magically become undone, exposing her long pretty neck, abundant cleavage, and braless breasts, as the rocking train caused them to do a jig within.

She watched me.

As her eyes bore into mine, she drew a breath deep enough to make her cantaloupe-size bosoms leap from her shirt.
    My lips twitched.

In the window beyond, the sun was going down, highlighting the twin peaks of her nipples in a fiery red orange.

My pussy throbbed.

A fog seemed to descend over the train. The voices of passengers and snatches of song from a boombox drifted faintly to my ears, and the aroma of a marijuana cigarette perfumed the air. She watched me and crossed her legs, then, ever-so-gently, she let them gap, sending into my view the full crotch of her jean slacks, beneath which all the pleasures of heaven lingered.

I gasped.

She gazed at me and precipitously smiled—her unique smile, half shy, and half assured. I fell back against my seat. Dizzy! On edge and on fire! I was experiencing something I hadn't before. It was thrilling. Yet at the same time uncomfortable. It was powerful, yet it made me feel weak. I turned away.

The next stop is Parkside Avenue. Parkside is next, blared the loudspeaker.

Without looking her way, and on shaky legs, I stood and moved towards the doors. I was grateful that the movement of the train and the horde of commuters camouflaged my unsteady sway, since we both knew that it was she and not the train that had seriously rocked my boat.

Quinn rose and followed.

As the train pulled into the station, she pushed up close behind me and pressed her cantaloupes into my back and planted one Timberland boot firmly on the right side of me, the other on my left, and wrapped her arms about my waist.

"Oh God," I moaned.

Faith was beginning to replace my doubts. As my juices flowed, I was excited to see the magic that was about to unfold. And suddenly, I knew that my flaws were perfect for the woman who was sent to love me.

TO BEGIN AGAIN

CHRIS ALLEN, MAUREEN COOKE, AND JIM TRITTEN

Elke, her face pressed against the airplane window, felt her husband Robert tugging at the sleeve of her ski sweater.

"Darling," he said, "the flight attendant is talking to you."

Elke looked past Robert to the male flight attendant — strong jaw, warm smile, and blonde hair with a hint of white. A good-looking man with green eyes in his late forties. For half a second, Elke's eyes shot up in surprise; then she shook her head — she wasn't that old. Men had been flight attendants for years now, but then they'd never been quite so attractive.

"Another Pinot Grigio?" he asked with the hint of a Teutonic accent.

"Please," Elke said. She glanced out the window again at the snow-capped mountains before turning back to Robert.

"Do you think it will have changed much?" she asked him.

"Mount Adelbert?" he asked.

She nodded. The flight attendant returned, handing Elke her Pinot, Robert a Manhattan, before disappearing as quickly as he'd appeared. A benefit of First Class — attentive yet subtle service. Elke watched the attendant vanish behind the curtain and then raised her glass of wine in Robert's direction.

"Here's to second honeymoons," she said.

"Here's to thirty years," he responded.

Elke tapped her glass against his. "A good thirty years."

Robert set his glass on the tray table. "So, you think Adelbert will have changed much?"

"Since 1991?" She laughed. "Yes, I'd have to say it's probably changed significantly. I'm guessing there might even be Wi-Fi."

Robert smiled at her, tilted his seat back, and closed his eyes.

Wine in hand, Elke released the lock on her seat and leaned back, allowing her mind to drift back to the tiny village tucked away high in the Alps. Adelbert was in the east of Switzerland, far from the crowds of St. Moritz or Davos. It was a quiet hamlet with world-class skiing and shopping, upscale dining, and secluded chalets — a perfect honeymoon spot and now their destination for a significant anniversary.

Our very own undiscovered gem, Robert had called the place.

Not entirely their very own.

Elke settled deeper into her seat, remembering the first time she'd been in Adelbert. It had been 1981, five years before she'd marry Robert; she was twenty-two years old and alone on vacation. She had been determined to spend two weeks focusing solely on her skiing, concentrating on becoming the best skier she could.

That's how she met Terry, her instructor at *Adelbert École de Ski*. Tall, broad-shouldered, tapered hips, with blonde hair, weathered skin, and pale blue eyes. Terry was the quintessential ski instructor physically, and his constant teasing and good humor made him the model instructor mentally as well. In short, Terry was the perfect teacher. One might even say the ideal man. For two weeks, every day, from early morning to late afternoon, they'd be on the mountain, where Terry brought Elke from a wobbly beginner, afraid of the bunny slopes, to a confident skier, eager, yet not quite ready to tackle the black diamond trails.

And at night? Off the mountain?

Terry once again was the consummate teacher, and Elke, the eager student. Even thirty-five years later, she remembered every detail: The charming hotel room with the leather furniture and antique desk; the bed, the feel of the soft wool blanket, the smell of the fireplace and the crackle of the fire; the touch of Terry's expert hands, his tongue teasing her. Terry had introduced her to being a fulfilled woman, and she had never experienced lovemaking like his ever again. She sipped her wine, breathed in ever so slowly, and shivered.

The flight attendant must have noticed her shiver, for suddenly he was there in the aisle, offering her a blanket. Elke grimaced and sensed the flush erupt in her face. She hadn't realized her memories were making a public spectacle.

She lowered her eyes to her lap as she waved away the attendant, sinking back into the past. Terry had been such an enthusiastic lover, passionate yet silly, making her laugh, even as she responded to his magical fingers that played her like a musical instrument, being satisfied completely and repeatedly. Afterward, they'd lie in bed, Terry still touching her, stroking her hair, massaging her neck and shoulders, and singing under his breath: "She'll tease you she'll unease you... she's got Bette Davis eyes."

She laughed now. *Bette Davis eyes. Not at all.* Elke Schmidt-Andersen was not that kind of woman.

Next to her, Robert snored softly. He was what society touted as the ideal husband, steady and rock solid. Always there to ground her from her flights of fancy. He'd given her a comfortable life; everything money could buy. No worries. She was grateful. Robert deserved her loyalty, and yet here she was, thinking not of him but instead of Terry. And that handsome flight attendant. She hadn't thought of Terry on her honeymoon. In fact, she'd given *Adelbert École de Ski* a wide berth, shocking Robert as she taught him what Terry had taught her.

Either Robert was not the student she had been, or she was not the teacher Terry had been, for her husband never quite took to skiing, or lovemaking, the way Elke had hoped. Although an efficient, purposeful skier or lover, Robert was not one to take risks or get silly afterward.

Now thirty years later, they were headed back to Mount Adelbert, and she was preoccupied with Terry: Would he still be there? Would he remember her? Would he look the same, act the same? Was he now flabby and bald? Elke shook her head; this was no way to head into her thirtieth wedding anniversary.

Unknown to Robert, she'd even booked lessons at *Adelbert École de Ski.*

She finished her wine, set it on the table tray, put her seat into its upright position, and glanced over at Robert, still sleeping; he had his eyes shut and his hands folded across his chest. To Elke, he appeared the same as the first time they met. Of course, his hair had grayed and thinned over the years, and he'd put on a few pounds, but his eyes were still the same warm brown. Kind and gentle. He was such a noble man, but their marriage had always lacked effervescence.

He stirred, then opened his eyes. "I had the impression you were staring at me. What's up?"

Elke took his hand and brought it to her lips. "Nothing. Just thinking what a lucky woman I am."

The Adelbert airport was just as Elke had remembered it: small, with only two baggage carousels; yet cosmopolitan, with people from Germany, France, and even Japan milling about, chattering as they collected luggage and ski equipment. Elke and Robert waited as the empty carousel went around and around.

"I hope they haven't lost it," Elke said. "That'd be a hell of a way to…"

A familiar and soothing Teutonic voice beside her interrupted: "In all my years, we've never lost so much as an overnight bag. I'm sure you'll be fine."

Elke followed the sound of the voice; it was the flight attendant.

Robert nudged her. "There they are," Robert said, pulling two matching bags off the conveyor with distinctive airline club identification tags and placing them at Elke's feet.

The flight attendant smiled and said, "See, we always keep our luggage with our passengers."

"That's all, right?" Robert asked her. "Nothing more?"

Elke shook her head. "All our equipment, I shipped straight to the hotel."

"Then we are good to go," Robert said, taking her by the elbow and leading her toward customs.

One final glance – bordering on a stare – at the handsome flight attendant in his sharp blue uniform with wings on his jacket. She sighed and then shook her head. The younger man was still smiling at her. Elke slid her arm through Robert's as they made their way through the terminal and outside, where the temperature was brisk and the ground covered in fresh white snow.

Robert put his arm around Elke's shoulder and pulled her close, kissing her hair. "Beautiful," he said, his breath fogging the air.

In the morning, the sun barely up and the snow fresh and powdery, Elke and Robert checked in at *Adelbert École de Ski*, a dark wood building with heavy doors, expansive windows, and decorative lattice work at the roofline. The two approached the sign-in desk, where a young pink-cheeked woman, with a regional white blouse and *dirndl* outfit adorned in silver, asked if she could help them. Robert asked for an instructor who specialized in "nervous beginners."

Elke shook her head in disbelief. "Beginner?" she asked. "After all the times we've been skiing, you think you're a beginner?"

"Simply being prudent," he responded.

"But, Robert, I've…."

"I know, dear, and don't think I don't appreciate what you've taught me; however, I believe that I'm entitled to *one* lesson before I venture onto the slopes."

Even though he was smiling, his words stung. She shrugged. Hardly an auspicious beginning.

Another young woman, dressed in a red and white ski jacket, grabbed Robert by the arm and danced him across the floor. Elke watched them leave, listening as the young woman chattered, "You're going to love skiing, I promise. It's just *so* much fun."

Elke turned back to the sign-in desk, "I don't suppose by any chance you still have an instructor named Terry Miller?"

"Terry?" The young woman raised an eyebrow and grinned. "Of course, Terry is still here. He is one of our most popular advanced instructors. But your husband indicated you were beginners. I have you scheduled with Rolfe this morning."

"He was speaking for himself. Terry was my instructor some years ago. I would like to continue with him. You know, pick up where we left off." Elke immediately regretted her choice of words.

"Ah, well, in that case, let me see…" She flipped some pages in the appointment log. "Ah, yes, Terry will be in at ten o'clock, in about fifteen minutes. He isn't available until this afternoon. Shall I re-book him for you?"

Elke again sensed her cheeks flush, and she lowered her eyes. "Yes, please." Just the thought of seeing Terry again wiped away the years and the petty annoyances with Robert. She giggled. She actually giggled. She hadn't laughed like that in years, not since her first visit to Adelbert.

Smiling, she walked away from the desk to look at a display of ski hats. At that moment, she heard the door open. Heart racing, her head shot up, thinking it might be Terry; maybe he was coming to work early, perhaps he'd heard she was in town, maybe….

But it wasn't Terry. Instead, it was the flight attendant. And he was walking her way, carrying a pair of skis over his shoulder — *what a hunk*. Turning away, she picked up the nearest hat and was putting it on her head when he said, "excuse me." Elke pretended to be preoccupied and again felt her face heat. She hoped the blush did not show.

"Excuse me," he repeated. She bit her lower lip to control herself and turned her head, an eyebrow raised.

"You were on the plane last evening, right?" he said. "One of my passengers?"

Eyebrow still raised, Elke said nothing.

"I want to apologize," he told her. "For my comment at baggage claim. About how we've never lost anyone's luggage. It was presumptuous." His smile lit up the room.

Elke continued to say nothing and realized her jaw was hanging open. She closed it by faking a cough.

"Are you OK?"

She smiled, "Yes, I'm fine."

He put down his skis, took off his gloves, and asked, "Should I get you some water?"

"No, thank you."

"Again, I'm sorry. I shouldn't have said that to you. I was tired from four flights in a row. I got caught up in the excitement of being off work. I wasn't thinking. Happens a lot to me — the not thinking."

He smiled, green eyes crinkling, and Elke realized she was smiling back.

"Friends?" he said, extending his hand.

Elke took off her glove and sensed an electrical charge as she shook his hand. "Of course. My name is Elke Schmidt-Andersen."

"And I am Caspar Schmidt!" He bowed from the waist, clicked his heels, and saluted her.

She raised a free hand to her lips and quivered. Stuttering, she joked, "So perhaps we are distant cousins?"

"Perhaps. My family is from Switzerland. And yours?"

"They emigrated from Bavaria. I guess there are lots of Schmidts all over the world."

"So we are, as you Americans say, no more than 'kissing cousins.' You look like you are in search of a ski instructor or a ski partner. New to the slopes?"

"Not at all. I've been skiing for many years. I just want a brush up on my technique, and I signed up with an instructor I know."

"Well, I will detain you no longer *gnädige frau* and wish you an enjoyable day on the slopes. Perhaps our paths will cross again sometime." With that, he saluted again, picked up his skis, and walked away.

She watched his high and tight posterior as he walked into the hotel lobby, the door opening and closing. Before she could even process the encounter, she heard a booming voice envelop her, "Elke? Elke Schmidt, is that you?"

She whirled. She'd have recognized Terry's voice anywhere. And there he was: as tall and broad-shouldered as she'd remembered. His sandy blond hair hadn't lost its glow; the light blue eyes still welcomed her into his embrace. There were new lines around his eyes, but happy lines. *He's glad to see me.* Elke couldn't believe how handsome he looked and how fast her heart was beating.

He raced across the room, grabbed her in his arms, and lifted her off her feet as if she weighed nothing. "My God, woman, it's been years! How have you been?"

Placing her gently back on the floor, he held her at arms-length, appraising her. "You haven't changed a bit," he said. "Same blond hair. Bette Davis eyes. The works. What are you doing here? Vacation? More ski lessons?"

She knew she had blushed, and he laughed.

"Seriously," he said. "It's so wonderful to see you."

Dropping her gaze, she said. "It's good to see you, as well. And, yes, I booked you for a lesson this afternoon."

"And afterward?" he asked playfully.

Elke shifted her feet and whispered, "I'm here with my husband."

Terry winked. "I don't have a problem with that."

He leaned down, kissed her cheek, and hurried off to the booking counter, leaving Elke standing there in the middle of the hat display to wonder what any of it meant.

Bette Davis eyes? He remembered. That's what it meant. He remembered. But did he still want her? And what did he mean: he didn't have a problem with that? A problem with what?

Elke paced the hotel room, waiting for Robert to return from his lesson. She couldn't get her mind to quiet. Terry had remembered her; he'd hugged her, lifted her high in the air, and flirted. Yes, he'd definitely been flirting. The mention of Bette Davis eyes. And that flight attendant, Caspar, was flirting with her as well. She hummed "Bette Davis Eyes" to herself. When Robert entered the room, she rushed to him, threw her arms around him, and whispered.

"Honey, let's do it, OK? Right here. Right now. Just screw my brains out."

"Screw your brains out?" he pushed her away from him and looked with a questioning face. "You don't talk like that."

"Make love then. Honey, I need you. Right away. That's all I'm saying. My entire body needs you. There's not a place on it or in it that doesn't need you. Please, honey, please. Take me. Please." She wrapped herself around Robert and jumped on his hip.

Robert dropped her off his side and disentangled her arms. "Elke. What's got into you? Give me a minute; I just got back from skiing, and I'm all sweaty. I need to clean up first."

Robert disappeared into the bathroom, and Elke flung herself on the bed, fully clothed. When she heard him start a shower, she slid out of bed and undressed, padding across the floor to the bathroom. She'd surprise him, climb into the shower with him, soap him up one side and down the other. It had been years since they enjoyed an intimate shower.

She turned the knob, but he'd locked the door. Why should that surprise her? Robert had always been prudish that way. Still, it was their second honeymoon, their thirtieth anniversary. Elke slunk back to the bed and lay there, eyes closed, tears starting, when she heard the bathroom door open. She waited for his touch and clenched her teeth as she felt Robert lay on the far side of the bed.

She rolled towards him. Perhaps she could salvage this yet. She kissed him and moved her fingers over his body. Feeling no response, she used all the techniques Terry had taught her so many years ago, including that little thing with her index finger; she tried to bring Robert to the level of excitement she and Terry had so easily achieved. Finally, Robert reacted, and she visualized it was Terry. She was amazed at how fast she satisfied herself and how she still wanted more. She wanted Terry, and she was going to see him this afternoon. Elke continued enjoying the moment, lost to her body, unsure how many times she'd responded.

Robert grunted, and she knew he was spent. Elke smiled and wondered if Robert had noticed she wasn't thinking of him. She rolled away onto her back. She saw Robert turn away onto his side and immediately begin to snore.

Elke got up from the bed and walked over to the mirror on the back of the bathroom door. She scanned her face. Some lines, some wrinkles, but not bad for someone in her fifties. *I still got what it takes to attract younger and hot men to boot.* One hand smoothed the skin under her chin and down to folds in her neck. *The years have changed a lot. But then, what did you expect?* She appraised her tummy — still reasonably tight. No kids, after all. *My body.* She turned sideways and saw her ample yet well-smoothed *derrière*. *Not quite like a young girl, but it's all yours, Terry.* Looking down at her legs, she smiled and thought she would show them off tonight with those black high heels with the red soles she bought for the trip.

She glanced at Robert sound asleep on the bed and went into the bathroom, singing to herself: "She'll tease you, she'll unease you… she's got Bette Davis eyes."

At three o'clock, Elke met Terry for the refresher lesson. The brisk air froze her exposed skin as they shushed downward on immaculately groomed trails through the pines decorated with hoar frost. Elke took in the crisp cold air and snuck glances at *Gaëlle Berg*, crowning the horizon at over 10,000 feet. The valley below was covered in pristine white snow punctuated by the frozen blue water of Lake Adelbert.

During the lesson, Elke studied Terry. He was joyous, funny, and attentive but focused more on his skiing than on her. She worried she'd misread the situation that morning and felt embarrassed, nearly humiliated that she'd thought he still had feelings for her. She flushed, remembering her interlude with Robert and how she'd pretended it was Terry touching her, satisfying her.

Terry motioned to her to stop at the next rest area, where they huddled beneath a building open on all four sides. Elke was chilled but exhilarated by the workout, emboldened to bring up the past.

"We certainly had a wonderful time all those years ago, didn't we?" she ventured, head down but peeking up at her former lover.

Terry threw back his head and laughed. "If by wonderful, you mean the best sex and skiing I've had in my life, then yes, we had a *wonderful* time all those years ago."

He put his arms around her, pulling her close and snuggling the top of her head with his chin. "We could have it again."

Elke's heart leaped. *He does have feelings for me.* Then she thought of Robert back at the hotel, so oblivious. The years they'd been together had not been bad ones. How could she even think about throwing them away? They'd built a life together. Her friends and colleagues. What would they think? How would they even know? It wasn't their business. It would be so easy. She saw a fantasy; herself skiing all day, just as she'd done so many years ago, then falling into bed. So easy. So… so magnificent. Like before. But then she thought of Robert back at the hotel.

He deserves better.

"I'm married," she whispered.

He smiled at her. "Doesn't matter to me."

"I'm here on my wedding anniversary. My thirtieth."

"A cause for celebration. You should do something special."

Elke nodded. *It was a cause for celebration.*

"Let me take the two of you to dinner," Terry said. "Tonight. DaVittorio? You do still like Italian, don't you?"

"That's a bad idea, Terry. We're on our second honeymoon." *The last thing I want is a threesome for dinner.*

"All the more reason to let me take you out. My treat."

"I couldn't do that."

"As friends, Elke," he said. "Old friends."

Still, she hesitated.

"I promise, I'll do nothing to make you uncomfortable."

She smiled tentatively. "I don't know. It sounds awkward, Terry."

"You know me. I won't make it awkward. It'll be fun, Elke. Trust me."

"OK, I suppose. However, you do not need to treat us. Robert and I are perfectly capable of paying for our own anniversary dinner."

Terry's booming laugh should have been infectious, but her stomach tensed as he took her hand, leading her back to the slopes.

She could have sworn he was humming "Bette Davis Eyes."

The moment they arrived, the *maître d'* seated Elke and Robert at a table in the corner against the windows with a premium view of Lake Adelbert.

Robert pulled out her chair and reached for her napkin to place it on her lap. Elke slapped his hands away.

"I'm not a child, Robert. I can take care of a napkin or two."

Robert's eyebrows shot up.

"I'm sorry," Elke said. "It's been a long day." *And this is going to be a bit awkward.*

He smiled and took the chair across from hers, looking out the window.

"Beautiful," he said.

Beautiful? Does he not know any other adjective? Beautiful. What about romantic? Gorgeous. Anything but the same old beautiful.

Elke scanned the room for Terry. Instead, on the far side of the restaurant, closest to the kitchen, she spotted Caspar, the flight attendant. *If I were a cougar, what I could do with him. Like that time....*

She glanced back at Robert, who was busy rearranging his place setting, moving his water glass closer to the plate, the wine glass farther, and moving his salad fork so it was at the top of his plate instead of to the side. For thirty years, he'd been rearranging his place setting, wherever they went. "Making it right," he said. *But why now? Why tonight? Couldn't he just be less anal?*

Elke noticed Robert's eyes flickering up and to her left and heard Terry's voice:

"There they are. The newlyweds."

Elke's heart rate increased, and she tried to suppress a blush.

Robert stood, extending his hand, as Terry approached the table; they shook. Terry grinned as he sat.

"You must be Robert," he said. "Elke spared no detail in

describing you, and I must say she did you justice. I'd know you anywhere."

Terry turned then to Elke. "He's every bit as handsome as you said."

Elke stuttered, but no words came out of her mouth. *What an ass I am.*

Robert smiled. "I'm afraid Elke told me nothing about you."

"Really," Terry said, his eyes back on Robert.

To Elke, it looked as if Terry were appraising her husband, his gaze moving appreciatively from Robert's face to his hands. Terry turned his attention to Elke.

"You told your husband nothing about us?"

Elke's stomach knotted as Terry once again turned to Robert.

"I was her first."

Elke felt the wind leave her chest empty.

Terry laughed, "Her first ski instructor. Years ago."

Elke's head swam as she struggled to regain her composure.

"I detect an accent?" Robert said. "American?"

"Idaho. Elke said you were from Boston. A professor now in Heidelberg?"

Robert nodded and picked up the menu.

"And do you enjoy it?" Terry asked.

Robert laid the menu down. "Enjoy it? I've never considered doing anything else, so, yes, I suppose I do enjoy it." He smiled at Terry. "And I expect you enjoy what you do?"

"Wouldn't do anything else. I had the opportunity to take over my dad's ranch, but I turned him down. I prefer the slopes to branding cattle."

These two guys are really hitting it off. I might as well be in another room. At least we've gotten off my past experiences with Terry. "How about we order?" she said to the two men.

"Absolutely," Terry said. "And the check's on me."

Robert and Elke both started to object.

"I insist," Terry said. "You are my guests. It's the least I can do for your anniversary, seeing Elke again, and meeting you, Robert. May I recommend the baby octopus in green sauce with the Bergamo-style polenta? DaVittorio is known for it."

"No, I think I'll stick with some *schnitzel* and *spätzle*," responded Robert.

Elke ordered the specialty of the house, as Terry suggested.

They enjoyed their food and two bottles of wine. Over *crêpes suzette* and *Disaronno*, Terry leaned back into his chair, clearly feeling the liquor, and looked at Robert with narrowly squinted eyes. "Robert, I think Elke and I owe you an explanation."

"No," Elke said, shaking her head vigorously.

Robert's eyes twinkled. "That you were lovers?" He leaned towards Terry and placed his hand on the other man's. "I'd already surmised that."

Elke felt as if she'd been caught naked in the middle of the street.

"Ahh," Terry said, "then it makes what I'm about to say all the easier. I still find her incredibly attractive."

"Yes?" Robert said.

"Terry," Elke said.

"But, Robert, I find you at least as attractive, if not more. And you are such an intellectual, an academic. A real challenge to me. A change of pace from the standard athletic types that haunt these slopes."

Elke glared at Terry and spurted, "I'm an intellectual."

Robert smiled at Terry. "I find you attractive, as well."

"Robert?" Elke's voice rose an octave.

Terry smiled merrily. "What are we to do with such a predicament? Or should I call it an opportunity?"

"Robert," Elke said. Neither man responded.

"Robert," her voice raised to almost a shout. She saw nearby dinners take note of the conversation and move close together and whisper.

"Robert, this is not an *opportunity*. This is not anything. Stop it."

Robert turned to her. "Darling, surely you've suspected or at least wondered. You're an intelligent, beautiful woman. Sexy. Have you never asked yourself why we are intimate so infrequently and why it takes me so long to be satisfied?"

Elke again felt the air rush out of her lungs. For a moment, she thought she might faint. Had their marriage, their entire relationship, been nothing but pretense?

"Elke, you must have known," Robert inquired.

"No," she said and glowered at her husband. "I didn't know."

"Does it matter?" Terry asked.

Elke whirled to face him. "Does it matter? That my entire life's been a lie? That my husband's gay? Yes, it matters. What in the hell's wrong with both of you?"

Robert got to his feet. "I see no reason to make a scene, Elke. This changes nothing. I still love you."

Elke stared at her husband in amazement. *Who was this man?* She watched as Robert helped Terry to his feet and said, "Beautiful."

Terry glanced at her. "Why don't you join us?"

"Join you?" Elke shrieked. "I'm not joining you. Not now. Not ever. Jesus."

Elke glared at the two men walking off together across the restaurant, Robert's hand resting on Terry's ass. *Great second honeymoon.* Robert was right. How could she have not known? Her hands covered her face, and she shrank back into her seat. All those graduate students over the years. Always male. The field trips. The choir practices. *I was an idiot.*

She got to her feet, planning. First things first, she'd get a separate hotel room, a flight home in the morning; she'd move Robert's possessions into the spare bedroom. She should demand he leave, but perhaps her own apartment would be better.

The waiter approached, bearing a leather wallet with green tassels. He handed the folder to her. *They'd stuck her with the bill. Could this possibly get any worse?* She settled the bill and headed out of the restaurant, but at the entrance, hesitated. She turned… awareness a bit foggy from the wine.

Caspar was still at his table, alone.

What do I have to lose?

Elke slinked back into the room. She saw him watching her and wondered if he had seen the scene with Terry and Robert. She didn't care.

Caspar rose and pulled out a chair. *Guten abend gnädige frau.*

As she sat, she extended her fingers to the top of his forearm, smiled playfully, and growled like a cougar. "Kissing cousins it is then."

Slightly different versions were previously published in: *The Criterion eJournal*, Vol. 8, Issue II (April 2017), 1231-1241; *Quail Bell Magazine*, June 19, 2017; *Anthology Askew Volume 004: Askew Communications*, Mandy Melanson & Dusty Grein, eds., North Charleston, SC: CreateSpace, September 30, 2017, pp. 73-89; *Love, Sweet to Spicy: A Corrales Writing Group Anthology*, Patricia Walkow, ed., North Charleston, SC: CreateSpace, January 2018, pp. 133-148. It was awarded Second Place in the New Mexico Press Women, New Mexico Communication 2018 Contest, Essay, Chapter, or Section in a Book.

THE OTHER MAN

RIZWAN ASAD

She came late, as she always did, through the fence gate that opened onto the back alley. Frank had given her a key to the front door, but she wouldn't use it, much to his frustration. He wanted so badly, just once, to come home from a long day of work and find Rupali waiting for him, maybe dinner on the table, or better yet, just her naked in bed.

But it was always just after twilight and she always slipped in through the back gate, glided across the little lawn and in through the sliding glass door without a sound, as though she were afraid of being followed, to find Frank eating a microwave dinner in his undershirt, his face pale in the light of a TV game show.

The only time Rupali had ever come into Frank's house through the front door was the first time she had been over, and she had left before nightfall.

They had met at the Pore Over, a combination bookstore and coffee shop downtown, around the corner from the garage where Frank worked. The other mechanics poked fun at him for drinking fair trade coffee while the rest of them subsisted on jet black Folgers from the shop's greasy coffee pot, but he had found that the expensive stuff was easier on his stomach and it gave him an excuse to duck out during lunch break.

Besides, the Pore Over was a haven for attractive women, a discovery that he would never share with his coworkers.

He had been topping off his venti Sumatran dark roast at the counter when he saw Rupali across the room. She had folded herself daintily into a leather chair in the corner and was completely absorbed in a book. Frank watched her dark eyes widen as they moved back and forth over the pages. She occasionally reached up to sweep a lock of black hair out of her face. A steaming teacup sat ignored on the little table beside her.

She was unlike any woman that Frank had ever been with. Her skin was dark and glowing, the color of his coffee once he stirred in a single splash of cream. The reading lamp that craned over the back of her chair used one of those antique style bulbs and the glowing filament reflected amber and blue in her perfectly smooth, black hair.

Frank made sure his navy work shirt was tucked in and that his hands were relatively free of engine grease. As he approached her, his heavy boots creaked on the bare wood floor. Frank stood before her and cleared his throat, but her eyes remained on the book. She turned a page and her left hand searched about blindly for her tea, but she still took no notice of him.

He bent at the waist and squinted to read the cover of the paperback she held in her slender, brown hands.

"Jh-um-pa...La-hi-ri..." he said falteringly, aware that he was probably butchering the author's name, but desperate for any way to get her attention.

Nothing of her moved besides her eyes, which rose to just above the top of the page, where they stopped and held him, suspended in a look of suspicion. Frank straightened and shifted his weight from foot to foot, feeling foolish as she continued to observe him.

Finally, she ended his torture.

"Have you read her?" she asked, angling the cover toward him so that he could see it more clearly. It was called *The Namesake*, and on the back was a large photograph of the author. Frank was shocked to see that she looked much like an older version of the woman holding the book.

"Ah...me? No," Frank mumbled. "I have a hard enough time with her name, I doubt I'd get anything out of her books. Good, is she?"

Rupali lowered the book to her lap.

"Very," she replied, smiling coyly.

Frank's stomach flip-flopped and he felt his palms go a little damp.

"Well, maybe sometime I could buy you a cup of tea and you could tell me all about it," he ventured.

She unfolded her small frame from the chair and slid forward until she was sitting on the edge of the cushion. The book slid from her lap and Frank watched it fall toward the rug, only to be snatched at the last instant by Rupali's impossibly nimble little fingers.

She set the book on the table next to her cup. The antique light cast shadows on her face that made Frank think she looked dangerous and bold. It excited him, but not because he liked bold women. His blood rushed because he liked to see the boldness flushed from their faces when he caused them to feel uncertain, small and fragile.

"Why don't you just rent the movie?" she asked as she reached for her tea.

Frank's brain scrounged up a retort that he felt would be witty enough, but as he opened his mouth to speak, her hand clinked lightly against the cup. When she sipped, he saw the humble little diamond twinkling on her ring finger.

Frank's gut burned with embarrassment and a simmering anger, as though she had tricked him, yet he knew that she hadn't.

"Maybe I'll do that," he said as he turned to leave, nearly toppling a stack of John Grisham's latest as he did.

As he reached the door he heard her speak out, her voice musical, but loud enough to carry over the shrieking steamer of the espresso machine.

"Let me know what you think of it."

∼

A week later she was at the coffee shop again, and she had indeed asked him if he had watched the film adaptation of *The Namesake*. Frank had not and was now kicking himself for it. The diamond remained on her finger, but she said nothing of her beau, and he imagined that she made an effort to keep her left hand inconspicuous.

It was that morning that he learned her name and he told her that it sounded like an Italian sports car, but in a good way. He told her where he worked and where he lived and where he grew up — all of which were within five miles of where they now sat and chatted.

Rupali, on the other hand, seemed to have been everywhere. She was born in India and studied in England, came to the States for work and then…well, she didn't say much about the rest, only that she was there in Minneapolis and liked it well enough, but she was bored.

Bored.

That was all that Frank needed to know. He had watched enough porn to know what bored housewives wanted, and nine times out of ten it was a plumber or a gardener…or a mechanic. Anyone blue collar and willing would do; and he would certainly *do*, if she would give him the opportunity.

"I think I'll rent that flick tonight, after work," he said. "You wanna come over and watch it with me? I make a mean Manhattan."

Rupali's face darkened and she batted her eyes in a way that drove Frank a little crazy. She withdrew a little notebook from her purse, a day planner. Opening it, she fingered through the pages as though stalling for time. Finally, she looked up and said, "What time should I come over?"

Frank told her seven would be fine, gave her the address and made a mental note to look up what went into making a Manhattan.

The opening credits of *The Namesake* seemed alright to Frank, but he had made Rupali's Manhattan strong and his own rum and soda stronger yet. By the time anything happened in the film they were tangled and tousling on the couch, breathing heavy into each other's mouths and ears and necks.

When Rupali ran her fingers through his hair, Frank felt her wedding ring snag and pull roughly and he smiled inwardly, thinking about the impotent and ignorant schmuck that was so poor at pleasing his wife that she was here with him. Now.

Her phone buzzed and she gasped and sat up, snatching it from the coffee table, pushing Frank aside. He groaned.

"We both know what's up here, Rupali," he said. "Let it go to voicemail. Tell him you were busy."

She only held up a finger and walked to the back of the house, slipping out the sliding glass door and into the back yard as she answered. He heard her voice as she talked to him and he bristled to hear how different it sounded. There was a softness and familiarity in her tone that he had never heard directed toward him by any woman in his life. She remained in the back yard for a few minutes and returned with her clothes straightened and her hair smoothed.

Frank patted the sofa next to him, but Rupali gave him an apologetic look and picked up her purse from the floor.

"I have to go. I'm sorry," she said. She pulled a compact mirror from her bag and checked her makeup in the meagre light from the television set.

"You sure about that?" Frank asked. He reached up and grabbed her by the hips, pulling her backwards and off balance until she dropped into his lap. Rupali gave a short, uncomfortable laugh and pushed his searching hands away from her body as she stood up.

"I'm serious, I have to go. But thank you for the drink."

She moved to the door and Frank remained on the couch, watching her. As she opened the door to leave, he called out.

"Rupali."

She stopped and looked back at him, eyebrows raised in question.

"Next time you come over here, leave that ring at home."

Rupali's eyes dropped to her left hand and then up again, but she did not look at Frank. She looked all around the room, at the spotted ceiling, the stained rugs, but never at him. She left quickly without saying another word.

Frank switched off *The Namesake* and found a rerun of Wheel-of-Fortune. The wheel clicked and the people clapped and ageless Vanna turned vowels and consonants as Frank finished his drink and listened to distant sirens crying lonely in the falling night.

It was precisely one week later when Rupali slipped in through the back gate and scared the shit out of Frank for the first time.

Frank's neighbourhood was iffy, but it wasn't the worst part of the city. Still, no one ever reacts well to finding someone suddenly standing next to them while they are watching television in the dark. Frank shouted and threw a glass, which missed and shattered against the wall. Rupali never moved, she only smiled and dropped her purse on the floor.

"What the hell, girl?!" Frank asked, his heart still pounding. "Don't you know how to knock? What if I had a gun right here? You could be dead right now!"

Rupali ignored the comment and sat down lightly on the couch, her grace incongruous to the weary look on her face.

"Did you ever finish the film?" she asked.

"The what?"

"The Jhumpa Lahiri story, did you get through it?"

"Oh, that. Yeah, no. I didn't. I think I dozed off," Frank said. "You can still tell me about it."

Rupali stared obliquely at the television, where Steve Harvey was dressed in an impeccable suit and tie, asking a family of excited Georgians about things one doesn't do in church. She made no reply.

"Jhumpa Lahiri," Frank said carefully. "It is a pretty name, isn't it?"

The corner of Rupali's mouth twitched and curled into a lopsided grin. She turned her dark eyes on Frank, and he saw that they only reflected; they showed nothing from within.

"So pretty," she whispered.

Twenty minutes later, when they lay naked and prone beneath his sheets, Frank felt the ragged scratch of her wedding ring against his shoulder blade. He would have complained, or mocked her, or simply slipped the ring from her finger and tossed it away, but he was preoccupied. It required all of his strength and focus to keep his body from trembling as she wrapped her arms and legs around him, drawing him into her as though she were the endless void of space that could never be filled.

It had been too long, he decided, since he had bedded a woman.

When he opened his eyes, it was long before first light. He was goaded awake by his parched tongue and lacerated back. She had already gone.

She continued to come, and she continued to wear her ring. Frank did not ask her to remove it again, rather, he resorted to grunting out oaths and insults against her husband in the moments before climax.

Without fail, Rupali would remain silent during his ecstatic tirades. She would simply gaze up at him with empty eyes as he said, "He can't make you feel this way!" or, "What kind of a pussy lets his woman run around?" and sometimes, "*This* is your home now! Don't think of leaving this bed!"

Frank would finish and collapse beside Rupali, never wondering how it had been for her, and she would wait until his breathing slowed and became even. Finally, she would say, "Anand is a good man, he does not deserve this pain."

Her response would be the same every time, no matter what Frank had said about Anand, no matter how much he had cursed or abused this man he had never met. And every time she said this, Frank would close his eyes and fall asleep angry, only to wake alone.

There seemed to be no pattern to when Rupali would choose to make a tryst with Frank, and she never appeared at the Pore Over anymore.

Every day, Frank went to work, suffered his whipped coworkers with their talk of their bland wives and idiot kids, came home, fixed a cocktail and turned on the television. He no longer paid attention to the gameshows — it seemed to be the same episodes over and over again. He only fixed his attention on the back yard, visible through the wide, smudged, sliding glass door. Frank would stare at the latch on the back gate until it was invisible in the dusk, and still he would stare, waiting to see the small rectangle of lesser darkness open up within total darkness to signify that she was coming. She would move across the lawn with matchless ease, the untrimmed grass bending and parting to allow her passage.

On nights that the gate didn't open, Frank slept fitfully on the couch with the light of the television colouring the chaos of his dreams. When it did open, Rupali stepped through and made her way to his bedroom, he slept as deep and cold as the dead, without dreaming, without moving, without rest. He woke each time in the bed alone, with only scratches and bruises, a bit lip, or a bleeding ear, to prove that she had ever been there.

Frank started skipping work more and more often. At first, he called in sick, faking a sore throat, coughing falsely into the receiver of the phone. Soon, though, he stopped calling and only showed up on certain days, always late, generally distracted, disheveled and out of sorts. He knew it would only be a matter of time before his boss told him to stop bothering.

It started one day when he noticed a man hanging around the shop. He was diminutive, quiet and furtive, with skin almost the same color as Rupali's. The man wore a wedding ring and sat stolid in the waiting room next to the dirty old coffee maker, fingering through a stack of old Auto Trend magazines.

Frank asked the other guys who he was, and Charlie said he thought it was a customer getting his Audi worked on by Grant, but Grant said the guy was waiting for Carl to change the oil in his Volkswagen. Frank felt suspicious and disgusted, then his disgust turned to anxiety and he skipped out before lunch.

Rupali had been showing up in his living room more and more frequently, and she came later each time. She was waking Frank from ragged and troubled dreams that he imagined were brought on by the stress at work and the three or four stiff drinks he had taken to pouring when he got home. His hands shook during the day, but rum smoothed things out in the evenings, so each night he began this regimen earlier than the night before.

One night he sprang awake when she touched his foot, propped up on the footrest of his easy chair. Her touch was like electricity and it wrenched him from his dreams with violent force. Frank rubbed his eyes and felt a coldness pooling at his crotch. He looked down to see that he had spilled his drink onto his lap. Tiny ice cubes sat melting and dotting his blue jeans. He looked up at Rupali, expecting her to laugh, maybe even mock him. If she did, he would take her roughly tonight, he decided, to remind her of who was boss.

But Rupali did not laugh, or even smile, she only gazed blankly at Frank in the blue-green light of the television, her face revealing nothing. Finally, she turned and shambled wearily to his bedroom, favouring her right leg. Frank tried to remember how long she had been limping for.

"Hey, what happened to you?" he asked as he entered the bedroom and switched on the lights. "What's up with your leg?"

Rupali was already in bed with the covers pulled up to her chin. She looked paler than before and there were dark purple circles beneath her eyes. He saw that her pants and blouse were already off, folded neatly on a chair in the corner. On the floor were a dirty pair of women's socks and one shoe.

"Did you lose a shoe?" he asked.

Rupali did not answer, only opened her legs beneath the thin blankets so that Frank could see her spread eagle and gaunt. He wondered if she had been eating enough. They never ate together; the only activities they engaged in during her visits happened right there in the bed. She bent her knees and the blankets peaked like twin mountains over the valley of her frail torso.

"Turn off the lights," she whispered.

Frank obliged before peeling off his wet jeans that now stunk of rum. He moved toward the bed but tripped over Rupali's errant shoe in the darkness, tumbling forward and landing hard on top of her.

"Goddamnit! Sorry, you ok?" he asked. But she made no reply.

He felt around beneath him, trying to decide where he had struck her, fearing he might have knocked her unconscious, but he felt only the mattress and his own cold sheets.

Finally, lost in his drunkenness and clumsy in the dark, he found the light switch and snapped it on. He was alone in his bedroom, his bed a mess of twisted blankets and sweat stained pillows. On the floor in front of him was a single, brown women's shoe. There were no dirty socks, no folded shirt and pants, no Rupali.

Frank picked up the shoe and went back to the living room, where he settled onto the edge of his recliner. He stared at the shoe for a long time, rubbing the smooth leather between his fingers, cradling the hard sole as though the shoe were a wounded bird. He was soon disturbed by a small, incessant sound and wondered if a rat had been wounded in a trap beneath the floorboards.

He sat straight and opened his eyes, realizing that he was caressing the shoe with his cheek as he rocked back and forth on the edge of the chair. The sound, a small, rhythmic squeaking, was coming from his own mouth, as he wept softly and alone.

She stopped coming over. A week went by, and then two, and Frank sat alone in his little house. He kept the front door locked and most of the lights off. Some guys from the shop came by to check on him, but they only knocked for a few minutes and then went on their way. If they had checked the back door, they would have found it open. They also would have been able to see Frank sitting in his easy chair, staring with bloodshot eyes into his own unkempt back yard.

He kept the television volume high and let the battery on his phone die. There was no one he wished to hear from besides Rupali, and she wouldn't call. She didn't even have his number.

Frank watched reruns of gameshows over and over and felt his spite grow as he watched the models in their long, sequined gowns, posing with dish soap or turning letters or beaming next to brand new convertibles. They were blonde and blue eyed and white-skinned. They were not Rupali at all, yet they became surrogates for his resentment toward her. Why had she left him alone in this house? Why did she refuse to take off her ring? She didn't even joke about her husband. That frigid bitch.

He was certain that she was with him now, with Anand, somewhere in their perfect little house with a nice lawn and a big front porch. They probably had a damned dog, too, a golden retriever or a chocolate lab that would sit and roll over and do all kinds of stupid tricks, just to get a treat.

Is that what she thought of him? Was he just another domestic animal for her, going down and staying down in order to get the treat that only she could give him? She had taught him to say the name "Jhumpa Lahiri" correctly, praised him when he got it right, and then bucked and writhed with ecstasy when he had said it between her legs, over and over.

That was it, he was trained to be obedient, subservient. Then she had become bored and abandoned him without a thought.

He sat in the airless house, fuming in his chair in front of the screaming television, slowly conceiving of a plan to find her, to find *them* in their cozy house with their mindless, drooling dog. He would come in the evening, when Anand was sure to be home, yes, he would come at supper time and knock on the door. Oh, the look in her eyes would be delicious. And would Anand be confused? Or would it simply confirm what he already suspected, but was too weak to face? Either way, Frank would not be pulling any punches, he would humiliate them both with one move and maybe kick the damn dog on his way out.

There was a news break and the dazzling gameshow models disappeared from the screen, replaced by an anchorwoman that could have been a sister to any one of them: she was all blonde, styled hair and red lips; perfect teeth and impeccable diction.

The woman on the news spoke beside a graphic that showed a chalk outline next to the taillights of an animated car. Words at the bottom of the screen read *Information Still Sought*. Frank came to attention as the face of the anchorwoman was replaced by the weary and grievous face of a dark-skinned man with a foam-topped microphone hovering before his face.

"I just want to thank the community for all their support," he said. "And to continue to ask that if anyone, anyone at all has information about the accident that took my wife from me, that they will contact the authorities immediately."

Now the words at the bottom of the screen read "Anand Ahuja: husband of hit and run victim." It was not the man that Frank had seen in the shop.

Frank slid forward on his chair, leaning as he strained his burning eyes at the television while the image dissolved once again and the screen showed the beautiful and smiling face of Rupali, looking as vibrant and mysterious as the day he had first met her in the coffee shop. Below her picture was the phone number of the local police department.

As the segment ended and the news report moved on to other matters, Frank continued to sit, unmoving. He blinked and his eyes felt like hot coals in his head. His hands trembled in his lap, despite the rum that already coursed through his veins.

Frank did not turn as he heard the latch on the fence gate turn and groan in the darkness of the back yard. He remained motionless when the screen door slid open and closed, and he did nothing more than close tight his tortured eyes when he felt her cold hands slide down over his shoulders and clasp against his heaving chest.

ABOUT THE AUTHORS

ASH ORLANDO

Ash Orlando (he/they) is a non-binary writer and performer from Sydney, Australia. They have published several short stories and poems, working mainly in the erotica genre. They can generally be found working on too many projects at once and attempting (and failing) to cut down their coffee intake.

Instagram handle: @say_please_baby

BRUCE PRATT

Bruce Pratt is an award-winning short story writer, poet, and playwright. He is the author of the novel The Serpents of Blissfull from Mountain State Press, the poetry collection Boreal from Antrim House Books, The Trash Detail: Stories from New Rivers Press, and the poetry chapbook Forms and Shades from Clare Songbirds Publishing. His fiction, poetry, drama, and essays have appeared in more than forty magazines, reviews, and journals across the United States, and in Canada, Ireland, and Wales. He is the editor of American Fiction.

CHRIS ALLEN

An archaeologist by training, Chris Allen has won several awards for her creative writing and editing. She specializes in composing humorous stories inspired by her chaotic life as a community volunteer, background player in film productions, fiber enthusiast, and equestrian. Chris lives in Corrales, NM, with her botanist husband on a small farm surrounded by animals.

DIANE KANE

Author Diane Kane dabbles in all genres and explores every aspect of writing and publishing. She measures her success by the friends she has made along the way. Her short stories and poetry have appeared in numerous Red Penguin publications. Kane is one of the founding members of Quabbin Quill's non-profit writers' group. She is the publisher and co-author of Flash in the Can Number One and Number Two, short stories to read wherever you go. Kane writes public interest articles for Uniquely Quabbin Magazine and newspapers. She published her first children's book, Don Gateau the Three-Legged Cat of Seborga, in 2020, in English, Spanish, French and Italian. She just released her second children's book, Brayden the Brave, in April 2021.

JIM TRITTEN

Jim Tritten is a retired Navy carrier pilot who lives in a semi-rural village in New Mexico with his Danish author/artist wife and four cats.

MAHENDRA WAGHELA

Mahendra Waghela writes and reviews stories/screenplays. His stories have appeared in Wordweavers (first prize for short story), Open Road Review, Orange Frame Literary Review, Woman's Era, Suite101 (55-word crime story prize), 69 Flavours of Paranoia, Apollo's Lyre (flash fiction prize), Vagabonds (short fiction anthology), 47-16 (short fiction and poetry anthology inspired by David Bowie), Twenty Two new Asian Stories 2016 (Silverfish. Malaysia) and Chicken Soup Books among others. Finalist in **MUMBAI MANTRA CINERISE 100 SCREENWRITERS 2014.**
Quarter Finalist in Best Cinematic Story 2018 Screencraft.org

Finalist in MUMBAI MANTRA CINERISE 100 SCREENWRITERS 2015

Competition Judge for RADIO MIRCHI-MAHARASHTRA TIMES PAINT MY INDIA 2050 POSTER Contest

MARTHA PATTERSON

Martha Patterson's plays have been produced in 21 U.S. states and eight countries and she's had many works published in books, journals, and magazines (Applause Theatre & Cinema Books, Smith & Kraus, Pioneer Drama Service, Silver Birch Press, Variant Literature, Swallow Publishing, and others). She has two degrees in Theatre, from Mount Holyoke and from Emerson College, and lives in Boston, Massachusetts, the USA. She loves being surrounded by her laptop, radio, and books.

MAUREEN COOKE

Maureen Cooke is a versatile write and editor with an M.A. in English, who studied fiction with John Nichols (Milagro Beanfield War) and Rudy Anaya (Bless Me Ultima), nonfiction with Harry Lawton (Willy Boy), and screenwriting with Matthew McDuffie (A Cool, Dry Place). Her work has appeared in college journals, California newspapers, and Baby Talk.

NICHOLE BLAKE

Nichole Blake enjoys writing all sizes and genres of fiction and creative nonfiction from her home in the SF bay area, CA. Her work has been published in Women on Writing, Sundial Magazine, and in the short story anthology 72 Hours of Insanity, Volume 9.

O'LABUMI BROWNE

Hairalujah is a memoir that portrays one woman's knock down drag-out fight to be. O'labumi Browne, amid other issues, fisticuffs a life of addiction, and abusive lesbian relationships. "Romance on the Ironhorse" is an excerpt from the memoir.

Ms. Browne has attended the literary workshops of Michel Marriott's, Soul's Sojourn Memoir Writers Workshop; The International Woman's Writer's Guild; Gotham Writers Workshop; and The Yorkville Writing Circle. (Dragon Della,) (a short story,) also from her memoir, has been published by Thereafter Magazine. Looking ahead, Browne is seeking publication for her upcoming memoir Hairalujah. She is a long-time resident of Brooklyn New York.

RISWAN ASAD

Rizwan Asad is a Toronto-based author of speculative fiction. Fantasy is kinda his thing, but every so often he feels like he's sleeping too well, and begins work on something a little darker. Aside from writing fiction, he is the creator behind the Saveur award-nominated food blog Chocolates & Chai.

His debut novella, Dio in the Dark, is scheduled to release in late-2021.

To learn more, visit: www.rizwanasad.com

Facebook: www.facebook.com/rizwanasadauthor

SANDI HOOVER

Sandi Hoover writes natural history essays, romance, thrillers, and poetry. She lives in Albuquerque with one husband and one cat, both her first.

SHARI HELD

As a Gemini, Shari Held tries her hand at many things. Career-wise, she's been a medical assistant, a procurer of industrial metals, a seller of imprinted sportswear, a web developer, a webmaster, and an adjunct professor. Currently she works as a freelance journalist, editor, and short story author. In keeping with her Gemini spirit, she writes romance, mystery, fantasy, and horror stories as well as nonfiction. Her stories have appeared in numerous magazines and anthologies.

When her fingertips aren't glued to her computer, Shari practices yoga, watches tennis, reads, creates jewelry, knits, and embosses metal. She lived in Italy for a while, but returned to her hometown of Indianapolis, where she lives with her husband and a clowder of cats.

SUZANNE BAGINSKIE

Suzanne Baginskie retired from a twenty-nine year career as an office manager/paralegal in a law office. She has sold several short mysteries and romance stories and twenty non-fiction stories to Chicken Soup for the Soul books and two Cup of Comfort books. Her stories appear in Red Penguin's Behind Closed Doors Anthology, A Heart Full of Love Collection, Woman's World, Plan B Mystery Magazine, The Wrong Side of the Law, two Daily Flash Fiction volumes, Woman's World Magazine, First Magazine, True Romance Magazine, Futures Magazine and Turbulence & Coffee. She is a member of MWA, FMWA and Sisters-in-Crime and The Short Mystery Fiction Society.

ABOUT THE EDITOR

JK Larkin (he/him) is a New York based writer and artist. He is the Editor and Literary Manager of The Red Penguin Collection, an anthology imprint which has published over twenty titles in the last year. When he is not reading, performing, or otherwise artistically involved, JK can often be found curled up on the couch with his best friend and cat, Ted.

ALSO FROM THE RED PENGUIN COLLECTION

What Lies Beyond: Sci-Fi Stories of the Future

I Can't Find My Flashlight – A Horror Anthology

The Beauty Within – Stories of Spirituality, Faith and Love

'Tis The Seasons – Poems to Lift Your Holiday Spirits

Stand Out—The Best of The Red Penguin Collection, Vol. 1

It's The End Of The World As We Know It – Apocalyptic Short Stories

A Heart Full of Love – A Collection of Romantic Short Stories

The Roaring '20s – A Decade of Stories

the flower shop on the corner – A Springtime Poetry Anthology

An Empty Stage – A Collection of Monologues

Behind Closed Doors – Mystery Short Stories

Once Upon A Time… – A Fairy Tale Anthology

Am I Overthinking This? – A Self-Help Essay Collection

Ernest Lived …and other Historical Fiction Short Stories

Stand Out – The Best of The Red Penguin Collection, Vol. 2

the ocean waves – A Summer Poetry Anthology

Made in the USA
Middletown, DE
19 August 2021